The Moonchild

Alan Richardson

Published via Create Space
January 4th 2019

Homage to Jack Parsons and Aleister Crowley
who knew about Butterfly Nets and Moonchilds
before I was born.
And to William Breeze for a whole lot of other things.

But mainly to Margaret
whose secret dances in the moonlight
when she was a little girl in Gibraltar
inspired this...

This book is (sort of) a companion to a previous novel, *Twisted Light,* in which Lilith's father, Kaspar O'Malley, tells his own story.

Sister Ndlovu and Robert Kirk also appear in my novel *The Giftie*.

Dr McHaffee, for his sins, appears in the novels *The Giftie, On Winsley Hill, du Lac*, and also *Dark Light.* I think I will grant him some peace after this.

The Merlin of Limpley Stoke made a very brief appearance in my novella about Merlins generally, entitled *The Fat Git*

Maisy Hobbes also appears in *Dark Light.*

Just saying.

Some published books

Geordie's War.
Aleister Crowley and Dion Fortune
The Inner Guide to Egypt *with Billie John*
Priestess - the Life and Magic of Dion Fortune
Magical Gateways
The Magical Kabbalah
The Google Tantra - How I became the first Geordie to raise the Kundalini. *new edition retitled as…*
Sex and Light – how to Google your way to God Hood.
The Old Sod *with Marcus Claridge*
Working with Inner Light *with Jo Clark*
Spirits of the Stones.
Earth God Rising - the Return of the Male Mysteries.
Earth God Risen
Gate of Moon
Dancers to the Gods
Inner Celtia. *with David Annwn*
Letters of Light
Me, mySelf and Dion Fortune
Bad Love Days
Short Circuits
The Templar Door

Fiction

The Giftie
On Winsley Hill
The Fat Git – the Story of a Merlin
The Great Witch Mum – *illustrated by Caroline Jarosz*
Dark Light – a neo-Templar Time Storm
The Movie Star
Shimmying Hips
du Lac
The Lightbearer
Twisted Light

Apparently Parsons or Hubbard or somebody is producing a Moonchild. I get fairly frantic when I contemplate the idiocy of these goats.

Aleister Crowley's letter
to Karl Germer, April 1946

This impasse is broken by the incarnation of another sort of force, called BABALON... [This] force is actually incarnate in some living woman, as the result of the described magical operation. A more basic matter, however, is the indication that this force is incarnate in all men and women, and needs only to be invoked to free the spirit from the debris of the old aeon, and ... into constructive channels of understanding and love.

The Book of Babalon
Jack Parsons

The Burney Relief from Baalbek, in the British Museum. It is known, contentiously, as the 'Queen of the Night'.

In My Name she shall have all power, and all men and excellent things, and kings and captains and the secret ones at her command. Seek her not, call her not. Ask nothing. Keep silence. There shall be ordeals.

The Book of Babalon

Her mother always taught her that she was a Moonchild and that there was no dark side to the moon but only a far side, with its own phases that no-one ever saw, and never understood. She said the word with a strong emphasis on the first syllable, extending it a fraction, as if the concept of *Moooon* was more important than that of Child.

Her mother also said that she herself was a *hierodule,* and she emphasised that too, explaining it to be a sacred prostitute serving the men who ruled this world, acting behind the scenes, exerting subtle and secret pressures on those who thought they were the Shining Ones.

Her mother, she was made to understand, was part of a secret tradition going back to the Old Goddesses of the Oldest Land.

None of these words meant anything to her then but she hung them up in a secret place in the far side of her memory. She wanted her mother to say: *Lilith, nothing you can do or say will stop me loving you.* Or *Lilith, you are the best thing ever in my life.* Or *Lilith, nothing and no-one is more important to me than you...* She craved nothing more than cuddles.

Instead she had to cling onto the words hierodule, sacred, secret and Shining Ones, hoping that one day, when she was a big girl, their meanings would crack open to reveal warmth and safety. Instead, when she was 7:

'Your mum is a junkie,' said a classmate, reading from a red-topped newspaper called *The Sun* that she had brought specially. 'She's a famous groupie.'

The terms weren't familiar. Her classmate took great and graphic care to explain.

'My mum is a lunatic,' she answered then, as she would always do later, because she could remember a woman with a face like wrinkled cellophane being carried off screaming, by strong men in dirty white coats whose hands were stained yellow by nicotine.

That night, after she had read the article in the newspaper which her classmate had helpfully left, she curled up on her bed and became very thin as she faced the wall.

That doesn't make her wrong though, she thought, curving into the blankets and pulling them over her head.

The doctor who came with the men in dirty white coats had a centre parting of blonde hair that swept down over his ears. He wore a dark blue suit with flared trousers, black shirt and light blue tie, loose at the neck. Lilith noted that he had pointed black shoes and no socks.

'I'm Doctor McHaffee,' he said. 'I'm here to help you.'

Lilith fought back tears, worried about her mum. She tried to push herself into the far side of her mind where there was greater stillness.

'My my my...' he whispered, after the screaming mum had been carried off down the stairs. Then he went and pulled aside the heavy red velvet curtains to let an acid sun burn into the room and opened an old sash window to get fresh air.

Lilith breathed it in. She had seen many strange men come into this room of late so this one didn't frighten her. The air felt good.

His face came very close to hers as she came to the edge of the deep cot that served as a bed and cage. He seemed fascinated by her dark eyes, the iris the same colour as the pupil. 'You are very thin and bent,' he said.

Lilith nodded. She was also hungry. Her mother was never interested in food when she was injecting. She injected because she was ill. Really, she was the best mum in the world.

'You are Lilith aren't you?'

Lilith nodded again.

'One of the neighbours downstairs told us about you.'

Lilith pulled back.

'You're not in any trouble. We need to help you. You are so very thin.'

She gave a quick nod. A new phase had begun. The thin crescent of light she was giving to the doctor (not much brighter than the luminous dial on her toy watch) was all she needed for the moment. He never knew that on that *far* side of her soul her mother sometimes spoke about, there was much shining. That side, which some would call the dark side, this nice doctor would never see.

'Come,' he said, putting out his hand. She took it. He lifted her up out of the cage – for that was what it was - very carefully, gently, so as not to break any bones and stared into her dark eyes again. 'Can you speak?'

'Time is...' she whispered in a shrivelled voice, prompted by something from that hidden far side.

'Time is what? Time is what, Lilith?'

Lilith bent her mouth downward like a clown's but kept silent. No need to say more.

'Okay, now... do you want to take anything with you? Any toy? Oh my goodness you poor thing... I don't see *any* toys!'

She reached to one side and grabbed a long cane stick that had a conical fine mesh attached and held it tightly with both hands.

The doctor frowned. 'Is that for catching tadpoles?'

'Butterflies,' she whispered, into his left ear, smelling the wax.

8

'My my my...' he mused again as he carried her down the stairs to his car. 'I had hoped to watch a man landing on the Moon today but I'm so glad I came here instead...'

In July 1969, Neil Armstrong's footprints had barely crunched on the dry dust of the Sea of Tranquillity when Lilith found herself on an emergency placement in a care home in Bethnal Green, in east London. They didn't know what to make of her. She was thin, somewhat bent and decidedly odd. She ate a lot, threw most of it up, and ate some more. Her skin was parchment.

The Matron of the house – it could scarcely be called a home – wore heavy make-up with bright red lips, large earrings and big hair. She felt she was in her trendy prime but knew that a clock was ticking. The children under her supervision were demons. Lilith herself was uncanny: she walked in curves.

Did her mother teach her anything proper? the Matron asked the Doctor. *Was she confined to that small cot for the past 4 years? No wonder she has weak legs. She is very odd. Little feet, like claws. Weird things happen around her. The other inmates are scared.* She saw the Doctor's concerned face, a very handsome face, and changed tone. *Poor little mite,* she added, *Poooor little mite* - but that last was more for the sake of the sexy Doctor and the funding authorities.

The Doctor noted that the Matron actually shuddered when she talked about her new ward. And he himself, behind his professional mask, squirmed at her use of the term 'inmate'. He jotted everything down while making a mental note to get this woman removed from her post as quickly as possible.

For Doctor McHaffee, who also felt that a clock was ticking but on career rather than biology, this was promising to be a great case study. Hopefully it would make his name like Freud had done with Anna O., or Jung with his Miss S.W. And failing all that he would contact the journalist Maxy Mack and sell the story to the *News of the World* about the celebrity addict and porn star Slicky Vicky and her neglected, mentally handicapped child.

'She whispers strange things,' said the Matron, noting that doctor wore no wedding ring and making sure he noticed her own bare finger. Such as: *Time is.* Or *Nine Moons.* Or *Earth is Mine.* The girl spoke softly, quickly, to herself. The Matron didn't catch them all and Lilith would never repeat, just curved away, sometimes looking behind her at no-one and nothing.

Dr McHaffee nodded and made a note of these gnomic statements. In fact he had a good idea where they came from. He had scoured the flat for clues as to the mental state of mother and child. The only literature he found was a bound copy of a nonsensical, heavily-underlined *Book of Babalon* in which he had seen some of the little utterances that Lilith had come out with. He guessed that this had been read out loud to her, or at least in her presence, frequently, with no normal conversation that she could respond to.

'They both need help,' he said.

'Shall we meet for a drink later and talk more?'

'No,' he said, sharply. 'I need to go to the secure unit to see her mother. Lilith said she has the best mummy in the world.'

'Pah!' said the Matron, snorting, as much at the rejection as the comment. 'They all say that.'

Of course, if this had all happened today in the 21st Century Slicky Vicky would have sold her own story and been on every chat show. Lilith would be lauded as an Indigo Child or Star Child, or even as a Black Eyed Kid, with interstellar origins taken for granted. As for her powers, which she had always kept well hidden from anyone but her mother, they would make her an internet sensation, although most would brand her a fake.

But this was July 1969 and Man had only just landed on the Moon and the world wasn't quite ready for Lilith yet.

She sat on a creaking chair that smelled of wee, in a large room known as the lounge. It was lit by two long fluorescent ceiling lights, one of which was flickering. On the old sideboard was a big lava lamp with a Dymo label saying that this had been donated by a local benefactor called Tom Driberg M.P. Most of things in the house - refrigerator, cooker, hoover, washing machine, electric kettle, record player and tumble dryer - were labelled this way, as if the benefactor was so bad he wanted the world to know he was really good. A large but empty budgie cage was hung in a corner. Other children in the home, out of goodness or devilment, released every bird the Matron had encaged until she gave up buying them.

The red wax inside the lava lamp was shaped like a melting skull and it rose and sank, casting a bloody glow up the wallpaper. There was a big black and white television in the corner and a programme on called *Mary, Mungo and Midge* about a little girl and her pet dog and mouse at the seaside. She'd never been to the seaside.

Lilith wanted to get into the screen and be Mary. She wanted a little dog and a pet mouse and have little safe adventures where nothing bad happened. The strange species around her – other children in care, nine of them - looked at her oddly. But at least they did look at her. When her mummy had visitors and they took their medicines together, sometimes sharing needles, it was as if she wasn't there.

Although the atmosphere was spiky and the flickering light was giving her a headache she wasn't too afraid. The children were scrubbed clean, as she herself had been scrubbed clean on arrival. The soap was green, the towels thin. She liked being clean but she ached for her mum, the best Mum in the world.

Poor Lilith. Despite her unearthly talents, she hadn't yet realised that all children thought the same. Here among the abused, neglected and unwanted, was proof of the infinite power of the Mum, the world over and for all time. The records and files kept for each child bulged with accounts of parental neglect, drunkenness, torment, mental cruelty, violence and abuse. They had been popped out into the world by men and women who were never capable of looking after them. Among the children themselves, as the Matron recognised, they would argue, attempt friendships, fall out and hate. They could take all the hunger and punishment in the world but the worst thing you could do was insult their Mum. *Take that back! Say sorry! I've got the best mum in the world!* they would scream, while punching, kicking and gouging.

Lilith might have been a Moonchild but at that moment she was also just a little girl who didn't understand much about the world on which she shone, and who desperately needed cuddles.

'Why are you holding that tadpole net?' asked a shaven-headed boy called Wayne who smelt of bubble-gum. He had a warty face and fat lips as if he'd been in a fight.

'It's for butterflies.'

'You're a nutter. I don't like nutters.'

He took the net and broke the cane shaft over his knee, throwing the pieces aside.

'Don't you care? Still got that stupid look on your face? Now I'm gonna punch you.'

The other children grinned. This was better than *Mary, Mungo and Midge*. In places like this, scapegoats were more important than friendships.

His hand drew back and Lilith closed her eyes tight. She clenched her own little fists and began rocking.

Behind Wayne, the lava lamp exploded, glass flew everywhere and the molten wax skull dripped onto the floor. The flickering ceiling light crackled and went dead. The children screamed.

The Matron and two assistants came running in.

'Who did this?' she shouted, treading carefully over the broken glass and flowing wax, reaching to the switch to cut the power.

'She did!' they cried in unison.

'Well *did* you, Little Miss Loony?'

Lilith opened her eyes to find the Matron's face glowering into hers.

'Yes. Yes I can...'

And gather my children unto me, for THE TIME
is at hand.

The Book of Babalon

She was a crushed butterfly. Her diaphanous white dress, from
the new Biba shop in Kensington, had a loose membrane
reaching from each wrist down to its hem. It clung to her
wasted body. She had been violent on arrival so they had not
yet managed to get her into the hospital gown. Plus the staff
were all afraid of what celebrities might arrive to make a fuss.
She was known to be friendly with David and Mick, John and
Keith and Terence and Jean. The Friern Hospital, formerly the
Colney Hatch Lunatic Asylum, had attracted bad publicity
lately and couldn't afford more if that lot turned up.

She stood in the corner, bent, coughing, hands clutching
her shoulders.

'I'm sick, doctor.'

'You're in withdrawal.'

'No I'm really really sick. I've got the shits. Feel my brow,
I've got a fever.'

'They're the symptoms of heroin withdrawal.'

'No, you stupid man, I really am ill.'

'What are those marks on your arms, your legs?'

'Scorch marks. From when I fell to Earth. I'm gonna throw
up.'

She did so, into the waste-basket of his office.

'You need to get me straight. I just wanna get straight.'

Dr McHaffee said nothing, yet his mind was racing. Should
he start her immediately on the methadone? Then try to

empath with her, absorb her world-view, try to link her with with the side of herself that she has not yet met?

Her face had been in many of the papers, although the woman before him was an emaciated, almost cartoon-like parody of those famous features.

'I'll help you. But we need to talk.'

'Just give me one. One last shot.'

'You know what they say: one is too many; a thousand is never enough.'

'Shut up you moron! What do you know? If only you knew…' She went to his desk and rapped on it, nine times. 'See? You don't understand do you?' Then she slumped into the corner and curled up, clutching her stomach, the waste-basket ready for more puke.

He saw his chance.

'Vicky, if I may call you that, I know that: *your way is not in the solemn ways, or in the reasoned ways, but in the wild free way of the eagle, and the devious way of the serpent, and the oblique way of the factor unknown and unnumbered.*'

She looked up. Her green eyes widened amid the cellophane lids as he continued:

'*And you the secret, the outcast, the accursed and despised, even you that gathered privily of old in my rites under the moon.*'

For a moment, McHaffee glimpsed both surprise and hope.

Because for a second, Vicky thought that he might have been an Adept, a Secret Brother, one who has known the Black Pilgrimage and who could mediate the mad energies flowing through her thinning veins. Then…

'Oh you bastard. You stole my book, didn't you?'

He opened the top drawer of his desk and brought it out, pushed it across. He had already photocopied it for future reference and memorised apt lines. It was rubbish, but at the same time priceless.

'Vicky, listen -'

'I am not Vicky. I am the Lady Babalon. Ba Ba Babalon.'

This was wonderful. There were archetypes galore in this woman. He would become honoured among Jungians and prince among the analysands. Then he'd start his own practice and get out of this dumping ground of a mental hospital. He lit a cigarette, a Gitane. It was actually from a packet he had lifted from her flat. He came over to the corner and offered her one, crouching at her level, seeking eye-contact, looking to begin the 'participation mystique' that was at the root of Jungian depth analysis.

'Doesn't the Lady Babalon say thank you?'

The faintest wafer of a thin smile, then:

'Thank you.'

Her hands shook, she inhaled deeply.

He could see how once she had been beautiful, and not long before. She had shoulder-length red hair, slant green eyes with dilated pupils and full lips over perfect teeth.

She sucked on the ciggy again and breathed out, right into his face. She knew all about men (and women) trying to participate.

'Vicky, why the butterfly net?'

She frowned. Itched. Wiped her running nose on her sleeve.

Because...because...

Then... remembrance. She exploded.

'Lilith! *Liiii*lith! Where is she?'

She was on her feet, pushing McHaffee to one side. He stood before the door and wouldn't let her through. She slapped and kicked him but they were butterfly slaps. Then she stood back and faced him, snarling.

'She is safe, Vicky. She has been taken into care by social workers.'

'*Why?!*'

'Because you neglected her.'

'But I've been *ill* you twat! I wasn't neglecting her, I was *protecting* her.'

'From whom? From what?'

16

'From people who are afraid of what she is. People who would destroy her.'

'What is she?'

'She is a *Moooon*child. **The** *Mooon*child.'

'Explain. I need to understand before I can make you well.'

Vicky then vomited and shat at the same time. She gave McHaffee a look that said it was all his fault.

'I'll get the nurses to come and clean you up and into new clothes.'

'Just one shot, please doctor, do me up. I need to get straight. Listen: *I am the blue lidded daughter of sunset, I am the naked brilliance of the voluptuous night sky. To me. To me.* Please, I'll do anything to you...'

Night times were difficult for Lilith. When you're a teeny tiny child, even if you are a Moonchild, Time is a scary monster. An hour is a day, a day is a week and a week itself is a major part of a lifetime. She knew that the world around waxed and waned (although she couldn't have used those words herself), but she didn't know yet how to make use of this. Her mummy had been gone for aeons, as she had once heard her use the term.

The other children completely ignored her during the day. They whispered, they kept their distance. No-one asked her to play. Lilith wondered if she should have let Wayne punch her. She decided that when her mummy did appear she would buy them a new lava lamp.

The children were now making a great fuss of the staff. The staff were charmed, they agreed that actually the little mites weren't demons at all, and probably just needed love. The Nursing Auxiliaries and the State Enrolled Nurses who staffed the place felt that even the Matron had softened toward them, and so their jobs were nicer and tea breaks longer.

'We don't have any problems with *them*,' said the staff at the changeovers. 'It's that Lilith who's the source of all their anxieties. Poor little Wayne is a nervous wreck.'

In a short space of time (as experienced by the adults), the new little girl became, always, *That* Lilith. It was almost a title.

McHaffee visited, but the staff had absorbed and echoed the Matron's increasing distaste. Anything to keep on her good side. In 1969, Matrons and Charge Nurses still had awesome power. The year before one of the junior nurses - a married man with small children - had been instantly dismissed for taking two aspirin for his hangover. No mercy, no turning a blind eye or a second chance. So when they saw the Matron's frosty attitude toward the doctor then their comments were as icy; they had bills to pay and a job in the NHS then was a job for life:

He's only visiting because he fancies her tart of a mother.

Something about him I don't like.

Couldn't he wear socks?

Or a narrower tie. Never trust a man with a kipper tie.

I'm sure he smells of Brut.

Never trust a man with deodorant.

He thinks he's so special.

Typical trick-cyclist. That Lilith needs firm discipline and not his stupid word-association stuff.

He doesn't understand that we're not allowed to show them love in case they get attached before they go away. Besides, how can you love something like That?

Their assessments of Lilith were hardly more approving:

She needs Largactil, that's all. 5 mls tds. That'll sort her.

Is that scoliosis of the spine, or is she too lazy to sit up straight?

Too lazy. Just stares at the telly with a little thin smile.

And have you seen her feet? I get ill just looking at them.

Did they bind them when she was a baby? Chinkies do that don't they?

Actually, between ourselves, and I know you'll think I'm a nutter but I think – only me, mind you – that she needs an exorcist. I've seen things move without her touching. Poor little Wayne is wetting the bed now, he's so afraid. I clutch this little crucifix when I'm near her.

The staff tightened their lips. One by one they bought little crucifixes too.

During the day, when it was on, Lilith sat before the telly watching *Mary, Mungo and Midge* wanting it never to end. Although she didn't know the concept of '2D' that's what she needed to become: thin and simple, in a bright cartoon world where all adventures were safe ones. She wanted a little dog and a pet mouse. *They* would love her. She would cuddle *them.*

But the nights within the care house became almost too much. In the darkness, before their own bad dreams, the other children threw things at her. It was not the items which hurt her, but the hate. They took out on Lilith all the anger they felt at their own abandonments and betrayals. Their target knew there was no point in saying anything to the staff. She knew that they would all deny it and somehow she would get the blame.

Sometimes she almost felt sorry for the other children, because the silent far side of her which was very very *very* old, understood all this. Besides, Lilith knew that she and *only* she had the best Mummy in the world and they didn't. Poor little people.

She could have done things to them, as she had done with the lava lamp. There was that other side to her that she could use, but it was scary. All she wanted was to be cuddled and safe, while worrying about her Mummy who must surely be ill.

Where is she? When will she come?

Because she was too afraid to stretch out and sleep, she sat upright, cross legged, back against the wall. She could see well in the dark and had good hearing; she knew when the others were all asleep and could relax. Quite often that was how the morning shift found her, curled up, in the corner, the sheets under her wet and smelly. They had an answer to that: a rubber mattress protector.

Yet she had stolen a knife from mealtime. It was sharp, with a long curved blade with two sharp spikes on the end. Slipped it beneath the mattress and the base of her bed. She had to hide it because if anyone saw they would say she was going to use it on Poor Wayne. They all called him that now – Poor Wayne - and cuddled him accordingly. Really, if Mummy didn't turn up soon, looming out of the night to swoop her up and take her away, she would stab herself with it because Mummy always said there was no such thing as death.

She had also heard her Mummy say once, reading from her magic book: *But my children will know thee and love thee, and this will make them free.* Lilith wondered then what other children there were, and if she had any brothers or sisters. But as she remembered the words now, in the uttermost loneliness of the night, she most certainly wanted to be made free.

She took the knife from under the mattress. What was that bit in Mummy's magic book?: *Call me, my daughter, and I shall come to thee...* If this didn't work, she would kill herself.

Mummy! Mummy come, please come!! she thought with all her strength, clenching her fists and jaw and every muscle in her little body.

The darkness in the room stirred. It took shape and substance. She heard footsteps. Breathing. It was not her Mummy, but somehow a chunk of the darkness had come alive and came straight toward her. Getting bigger and bigger until it towered over her.

'Time is,' Lilith whispered, because even at this last moment of her life she didn't want to wake the others.

'Time is 11 o'clock, you funny little girl. Time you should be asleep.'

Darkness had a woman's voice, very husky but like a song.

Darkness gently took the knife out of Lilith's hands and put it out of reach.

Darkness said: 'You must be Lilith.'

And Darkness smelled warm and safe.

'I'm Sister Ndlovu, the night nurse. See me?' she asked, shining a little torch onto her own face. 'But you can call me Mary.'

Lilith had never seen a black person before.

'And I know what you need, more than anything...'

Lilith stiffened as she was picked up, removed from the corner by strong arms. But she was picked up and not grabbed. The night nurse whispered, didn't snarl or sneer.

'Relax, little thing. Snuggle into me. Don't you know how to snuggle?'

'I'm wet,' said Lilith, wanting to cry.

'Who cares. Wet away. I've got a magic power that tells me when a little girl needs cuddling and that's what you're going to get. I will sit here all night and give you the best cuddle in the world.'

And Lilith's bent little frame fitted into Sister Ndlovu's curves perfectly. And Sister Ndlovu's big soft hands cushioned Lilith's head against her breast and her whispers made a noise like the sea.

I shall provide a vessel, when or whence I say not. Seek her not, call her not. Let her declare. Ask nothing. Keep silence. There shall be ordeals.

The Book of Babalon

Although he would never admit it until years later, and then only in his cups, Lilith was always beyond McHaffee. If he was circling Vicky, as a kind of Mercury around her Sun, then Lilith was orbiting in the farthest depths of space beyond Pluto.

This was 1969, and children in England were still at the stage where (as far as his social class was concerned) they should be seen and not heard. Or packed off to boarding school 'for their own good'. This was decades, remember, before similar mites were left to rot in corners with game consoles, learning to grow up alone in cyberspace with dancing pixels for company.

To be fair, he did try. At first he thought he might have a phenomenon on his hands like Victor, the Wild Boy of Aveyron who in 1800 had been rescued from a solitary upbringing in the forests. Despite the best efforts by the good and kind, the only words the boy ever did speak were *lait,* meaning milk, and *Dieu*, meaning God.

Then he decided that it was better to view Lilith in terms of autism. That was not a new concept in 1969, but there was very little public awareness. With that diagnosis, he would refer her to a specialised doctor in a specialised place, while mentally washing his hands of her on all sorts of levels.

He suggested this diagnosis to Vicky, on one of her more lucid moments.

'I think your daughter might be autistic,' he said, hoping to impress her with his insight.

She laughed. She could see right through him.

'I don't know what that means. She's *the* Moonchild, that's what you have to know...'

'*What* is a Moonchild? You can't just label her and forget her.'

Vicky started to quiver. The quiver developed into a shake.

'Do that as much as you like Vicky but I'm not giving you what you want. You're not o'd-ing.

She stopped, closed her eyes, opened them. There was almost a dreamy look on her face. Then she sighed:

'A Moonchild is a Great Soul. Brought into incarnation for a reason.'

'What reason?'

'You will understand one day.'

He didn't understand that day, however.

'I think she's autistic.'

'Oh you stupid man. Lilith is, actually and truly, in all honesty, the bleedin' Messiah. A female Christ. And this time we women will get it right. Glory Ha-lle-looby loo-yah.'

He didn't get any sense from her after that. He could only comment in his journal: *Patient started laughing uncontrollably. Session terminated.*

That same day he drove across the Thames and spoke to the Matron, asking her three set questions that he got from an article by Bruno Bettelheim wherein the concept of unloving "Refrigerator Mothers" was mooted:

'Matron, does she: Frequently repeat set words and phrases? Is her speech monotonous or flat? Does she prefer to communicate using single words?'

The Matron bristled. He didn't know why she bristled or why she fingered the crucifix.

'She says nothing beyond those early words I mentioned. Yet I know she understands everything. I think she's got that daylight reversal syndrome. Sleeps most of the day, or pretends to. Go on, try and speak to her. Take a cup of tea in with you, I've got an important meeting now. Sorry.'

They shared a look. Daggers were involved on an astral plane of antipathy. He noticed that the other staff were glaring. They wore crucifixes too.

My my my... he sighed, and as he went in to see Lilith a little boy with a warty face kicked him in the shin. *Ooh – thank you very much!* was his awkward response.

Lilith sat before the television. It wasn't even switched on yet she seemed engrossed. He hadn't the slightest idea how he might attune himself to this creature. The room was empty, the other children elsewhere. It was as if an exclusion zone had been created.

He hummed and hahed, and didn't at all feel like a highly trained, super-professional with amazing, radical insights into the human mind and the psyches of troubled women.

'I've seen your mummy,' he said, and that finally got her attention. Her dark eyes bored into his. 'I'm looking after her, Lilith,' he added, using her name, looking to curry favour and get her attention.

'When will she come?'

'Soon,' he lied.

Her eyes on the screen again. In truth he was glad she looked away. He began to get the faintest sense of the Matron's unease.

'Do you have any friends here?'

She nodded.

'Who?'

'Sister.'

McHaffee was wrong footed. Should he play along or should he confront? Either might work with adults but with a vulnerable child? Still, he would have her re-directed to other professionals soon, so he might as well say, as gently as he could:

'You don't have a sister.'
'She's a night nurse.'
'Oh! What is her name?'
'Mary. Mary Endlove.'
'What is she like, your friend?'
' She has black skin. She cuddles me.'
'Lilith, what does -'
'I'm tired now. Time is. I'm going to sleep. '
So saying she curled up in the chair and did so.

'Matron, I'd like to speak to one of your staff about her relationship with Lilith. A night nurse.'

'We don't have night *nurses*. We rotate one member of staff in a duty room at the end, but none of them are actual *nurses*, none of them are qualified, they're just nursing auxiliaries.'

'That must be who she meant. Called Mary Endlove. Could I speak to her? Please?'

The Matron frowned.

'We don't have anyone by that name. Not even a 'Mary'.

McHaffee frowned.

'Lilith said she had black skin.'

'I would *never* app- I mean, there is no-one of *that* sort here!'

Their frowns matched. Their thoughts ran on parallel lines which would run through infinity and never meet:

Matron thought in terms of a demonic presence summoned from the darkness. For her, dark was Bad. The other side of the moon was dark and Bad. The best astronomers in the world would never get her to understand that there is no dark side to the moon

McHaffee, for all his faults, believed that there was no dark side to human nature, only aspects that we haven't explored. In his mind he thought in terms of the exquisite symbolism: a scared and lonely little girl creating a comforting dream-figure from the night called Sister Endlove.

Jung and Laing never worked with children as far as he knew. His hand-washing could wait a little longer. He would try harder with Lilith.

Three more sessions perhaps.

Adults were his metier, as were dreams and torments and archetypes. Two years before he had spent some time with R.D. Laing at the Kingsley Hall, where they accepted schizophrenia as a state of magical or even shamanistic reality and tried to enter the waking dreams of the patients. They sought to allow the people enough room to explore their own madness and chaos. Patients and therapists lived together but McHaffee was accused of getting too close to a couple of the younger women. He denied it, told Dr. Laing that this was a classic case of transference, that he was dealing with active and passive apperceptions, projection and counter-projections. That particular shaman, however, had no time for McHaffee's excuses or his underlying Jungian passion.

'You don't belong here Eric. Face up to it. You need to become a wanderer in the wastes for a while.'

McHaffee agreed, even though secretly he thought that Laing was simply jealous. So yes he *would* wander. And one day he *would* persist until the end and fashion his own psychotherapeutic school.

At that moment though, in the vast Friern Hospital with his own set of rooms in the West Wing, he still felt he was about to sound all the right notes with respect to Vicky.

But with Lilith, on the other side of the Styx-like River Thames, he was only gurgling.

Three more sessions, no more. He didn't want to start circling a plug-hole.

The next day, at the hospital, Vicky attacked him. She seemed perfectly calm and affable when she entered the room and gave a cheery wave to the male nurse who had escorted her.

She even gave a cheery, hand-close-to-chest wave to McHaffee. Just as he responded likewise she slapped his left cheek and then his right.

McHaffee didn't believe in violence. As a young man he had spent time with Quakers, and absorbed their notion that there is never justification for violence. Now, in the medical profession, he wouldn't even use the chemical cosh on the most disturbed of patients. Over the years, this had won him no friends among the embattled nurses on the wards. They knew that he would soon leave in his fine car after a 30 minute assessment and leave them to re-enact the Battles of the Somme for the next few hours until their shifts ended.

'Vicky...'

'I am Babalon. Ba Ba Babalon. The Lady Babalon.'

'Then Babalon, I'd like you to apologise.'

'Lady. Lady Babalon.'

'*Lady*, then...I thought you liked me.'

'Red cheeks, watery eyes, quivering...A typical man. You're too full of yourself.'

She looked dreadful. It was difficult to match this wrinkling stick-insect with the smooth, slim lines of the scandalous mannequin who had glided along the catwalks of London and Paris, showing the latest fashions for the gilded ones. David Bailey had said that the camera loved her, that she couldn't take a bad photo if she tried. McHaffee knew he could make a large sum of money if he took a photograph of her now.

In fact she looked as she had just described him: small blotches of bright red skin stretched over her angular cheek bones, pale white face, running nose which she wiped on her gown. He offered her a box of tissues but she threw them aside.

'You are so middle class, Son of Haffee.'

'And you are? What class are you?'

'I am beyond time and anything you could understand. I am from the intra-class: I exist in the cracks of society, the fissures of the world. I am a lubricant and a glue. I hold the worlds together.'

McHaffee had no answer to that.

Should he mention Lilith? Or ask about the father? There was no mention in any of the newspapers that she even had a child. This stuff about her daughter being the Messiah was interesting but no more than part of *zeitgeist,* the spirit of the times. In 1969 the world was filled with gurus and maharishis and mahatmas and bhagwans and very ordinary British men who became the voices of interplanetary parliaments or confidants of the space people.

Yet Vicky never asked about her daughter. Perhaps she really was one of those Refrigerator Mothers that Bettelheim described. Or perhaps the chill came from her existing in a stratospheric level high above 'normal' people, catching sunlight in the absolute cold of outer space but showing all her bones beneath her translucent skin.

'Poor, poor little man.'

'Why am I poor?'

'Because you don't know what to do with me.'

'What would you want me to do?'

'Get me straight. Give me heroin.'

'No.'

There was a long cold silence. He watched her carefully from the other side of his desk in case she was about to slap him again.

'The nurses think you're great. You never attack *them*. You flirt. Probably hoping one of them might get you some stuff.'

'I don't need stuff. Well, just a little. I'm not a junkie. I've been ill. But I'm also the Lady Babalon. I *am* great. I *do* flirt. Do you want me to flirt with you Doctor? Do you want to crack me open? There's a little blonde nurse on the second floor who's got the hots for you. I've heard she's bought you some socks.'

He frowned, though he shouldn't. This was getting absurd.

'This is getting absurd,' she said.

This shocked him. Had he spoken out loud? Had she read his mind?'

'I read your mind.'

'We will finish now Vicky. Same time tomorrow.'

'Tomorrow, bring little squares of paper, all numbered from 1 to 77. Then I'll *really* show you something.'

During those nights Lilith gained strength from the cuddles of Sister Ndlovu. Or Sister Mary as she liked to call her. Mary was actually her own middle name and she decided that one day, when her mummy came, she would insist on calling herself that. And she'd get a little dog and a little mouse. Not much to ask, was it?

Her mummy, according to the whispering staff, was rich and famous. *Why was she dumped here?* they mused. *And who's the father?*

It was 1969 and the country still thought that paternity and marriage were important. This was still all beyond Lilith of course, but one day, when she and her mummy were strong again, she would ask all sorts of things and learn all sorts of things.

Meanwhile, in the darkness, she found her own strength and needed shorter cuddles from Sister Mary. She also stopped wetting the bed and so ripped off the plastic protector. When she gave it back to the morning staff they called her a Little Minx and wouldn't look at the dry sheets which explained.

Sometimes she would sit before the huge telly and *Mary Mungo and Midge* would appear, though for the sake of the other children she kept the sound off. Once, one of the night staff had seen this but left her alone; then told everyone how the Minx had just been sitting in the dark before a blank screen all night.

She ate breakfast alone, every morning, then went back to her dry bed, or curled up on a couch to sleep after saying

'Time is'. Or pretend to sleep. She was never going to cry like the other children often cried. Sister Mary had told her that she wouldn't be here much longer, whereas the rest of them would be here for nine moons at least. Or even nine times nine moons if nobody wanted them.

Poor things.

'Poor thing,' said Vicky when she saw McHaffee with his 77 squares of paper on his desk, each one about the size of a postage stamp, each one numbered consecutively.

'Why am I a poor thing?'

'Too eager to please, doctor. Celebrities like me meet your sort all the time. You get boring very quickly.'

That stung him. He had a life long fear of being judged boring. Also he was having to suppress the idea that she could see deeper into him, than he could into her.

'Okay then *Vicky*,' he almost hissed, jabbing his face forward, showing that he was not going to do the Lady Babalon role play with her today. 'Tell me *Vicky* what these are for?'

'Like tarot cards. Do you know tarot cards?'

'Yes. Of course.'

'Do you know the *Book of Thoth* or the Waite pack?'

'No.'

'Then you don't know the tarot.'

'Listen, I'm not into games today. What do I do with these?'

She pulled her chair to the desk and with the flat of her hands shuffled the pieces around, never taking her eyes off his, grinning.

McHaffee was intrigued. If he could only look at her eyes alone, deep and green like an alien sea, he might think she was beautiful instead of a wasted insect-woman.

'Now think of what you want to know most in all the world and worlds. Are you doing it? Oh yes I can see from those two furrows in your brow!'

'So?'

'As they say, pick a card, any card. What number is it?'

'16.'

'I thought it might. Listen and learn: *And thereafter madness, all in vain. Thus it has been, multi-form. How thou hast burned beyond.* Ooh I bet that's shaken you, Doctor Mirabilis!'

'From your Book of Babalon no doubt. Have you memorised the whole thing?'

'Memory has nothing to do with it. It flows through my blood. One day it will flow through the blood of all women and they won't use Tampax to stop it. Do one more, ask Babalon for some more advice.'

'Vicky I -'

'Just do it you stupid man, and lose your boring soul.'

'Okay then... 24.'

'Oh the Lady is never wrong. That verse says to you: *Seek not the end, I shall instruct thee in my way. But be true. Would it be hard if I were thy lover, and before thee? But I am thy lover and I am with thee.* I always knew you fancied me.'

'I don't. Really I don't.'

And that was the truth, just then. She was scrawny, marked, unwashed and – dare he as a psychiatrist say it – mad?

'I'm not mad.'

He had planned to talk about the Shadow and how an identification with it, in the shape of Lady Babalon can produce amoral, inflated craziness. But somehow this didn't seem to be relevant to Lilith. Instead, they glared at each other. People did that a lot in 1969 when the English hadn't yet learned the simple social skills that didn't involve talking about the weather or sport.

'Vicky, I'm not playing this tarot game any more.'

'Frightened you didn't it? Spot on, old chap, old bean.'

'Now tell me about Sister Endlove.'

Vicky rocked back in her chair, her eyebrows rose. She scratched at the dry skin on her brow. The merest hint of respect came into her eyes.

'Where did you hear about *her*?'

'Lilith told me. She's visited in the night. Sister Endlove doesn't exist of course, so where did she -'

Peals of laughter from his patient, bending at the waist.

'Oh bless. Endlove, Endlove, that is so sweet. It's *Ndlovu*, actually,' pronouncing it correctly and then spelling it as McHaffee wrote it down. 'One day you'll learn about Sister Ndlovu. So will the whole world. But not yet. Now get me something I can take and we'll be friends for life.'

'No. You never show the slightest concern about Lilith.'

'Not now, no need, not if Sister Ndlovu is protecting her. She's got her own destiny to sort.'

'Vicky...'

'Oh I'm bored now, so very very bored. Ooh is that the time? Must fly. Lady Babalon is leaving the building....'

McHaffee sat in his office looking at the snowstorm of 77 flakes. He was tempted to do that augury again, using his own photocopy of the *Book of Babalon.* He had read everything Jung had written about synchronicity, including his own auguries with the I-Ching, so he wasn't dismissing the experience he just had. But for the first time he began to wonder if the gold he had found via Vicky was just faery gold, likely to disappear when he blinked.

There was a hesitant knock on the door.

'Come!'

The door opened partially. A female hand came through, holding a pair of long, ludicrous psychedelic socks, dangling them like the fish-bait they were.

'Nurse Hawkins, I presume.'

She followed, still in uniform, very curvy and fetching. Spiky blonde hair and a wicked smile. McHaffee realised that

32

he'd had enough of archetypes and goddesses and sacred myths and time-wasting *soi disant* celebrities. The Swinging Sixties were coming to an end soon and he really should lighten up a bit.

'Lock that door Miss Hawkins and join me on the couch...'

And this is my book, that is the fourth chapter of the Book of the Law, He completing the Name, for I am out of NUIT by HORUS, the incestuous sister of RA-HOOR-KHUIT.

The Book of Babalon

If McHaffee had been alive today he could have summoned answers from his i-phone, tapped queries into his laptop or verbally questioned any number of home Hubs that would flash lights and tell him much of what he needed to know. In 1969, however, he relied upon serendipity and synchronicity for all those crucial insights that he couldn't find at the nearest library. It was in Watkins bookshop in Cecil Court that he saw a glossy paperback screaming at him to come in and buy. So he went in and bought. Over the years he had come to trust these apports into his awareness and felt that his secret Master, Carl Gustav Jung, would heartily approve.

The shop owner, a small, bird-like man with a neat tweed suit and red bow tie, could see that his potential customer was agitated: he had the look of a man who felt that he might find the Holy Grail - if only he asked the right questions. Even so he had to advise:

'Do you *really* want to lose yourself in the *Confessions of Aleister Crowley?*'

McHaffee did. He made a living via confessions. Just flicking through the index of this large tome he could see that it might explain all manner of things with respect to Vicky and Lilith.

'Do you know the editors? - Symonds and Grant?'

'Grant is often in here. He's a Londoner. He was Crowley's secretary toward the end.'

'Would he know anything about something – an energy or a deity - called Babalon?'

'There's no-one better to ask...'

Outside the shop, his date was waiting patiently.

'Is that for me?' asked Nurse Hawkins brightly. 'Is it hard-core porn?'

For a moment he had almost forgotten she was there. He'd never seen her out of uniform before and somehow she didn't seem quite so engaging.

'No,' he said, showing her the title.

She shrugged, turned her mouth down. The book looked boring and she wasn't a reader.

'Come on Eric let's go and see *The Gypsy Moths* at the Odeon. Burt Lancaster and Deborah Kerr. All about skydivers. I've always wanted to skydive. Haven't you?'

'No. I can't stand Burt Lancaster. If he'd spelled his name with an *e* instead of a *u* he'd never have got famous. He's not an actor but a *re*-actor.'

'Oh you're so witty,' she lied. 'But would you skydive with *me*? There's a place in Surrey that will teach us. Would you? Will you? Can you?'

'No.'

'So what *do* you want to do, Eric? What do you really *really* want to do now?'

He knew from her tone that she too was finding him boring and would probably finish it soon. But he really *really* wanted to read this book and then meet Kenneth Grant.

For the past year, Dr McHaffee had been the most hated member of staff in the Friern Hospital. As there were over 300 on the nursing side alone, this was quite an achievement. It was whispered that he had provided investigative journalists with hard details about the regime. To outsiders, it was not that there was overt or even covert cruelty, but a complete lack of entertainment for middle-aged schizophrenic patients and nothing to do for the very many elderly. All of whom, the innovators argued, who would be far better served in the community. Questions were raised in parliament. The Physician Superintendent was lambasted by the great and the good of this land, many of them ermine clad.

The next day the Physician Superintendent, a bearded presence known to all within the hospital as God, had given McHaffee a great and good lambasting in return. God knew that McHaffee would never be happy until places like Friern were closed. He was fresh off his mater's tit. What did *he* know about *anything?* This dangerous 'care in the community' nonsense had always been part of the young doctor's flag-waving since he first arrived, highly recommended.

'I've never liked you, McHaffee. You might want to cut your hair and wear socks and look like a doctor instead of a bleedin' hippy. A lot of folk here think that *you're* the mad one.'

The bleedin' hippy had heard this before. In truth he had not given the journalists anything or even met them but he was happy to be the scapegoat. He could see the way the world was turning:

God, before whom he stood within the uppermost room in the asylum, had once done bold things in France during the Normandy Landings 25 years before. Or so he always hinted. McHaffee, who had a keen nose for bullshit, believed that God was a liar. Nowadays a few clicks on a lap-top or even a phone could confirm or expose all sorts of things about a person. But in July 1969, God could still dissemble.

'We've had Dave Dee, Dozy, Beaky, Mick and bloody Tich out here trying to visit your new patient. The rest of the patients are singing *Legend of Xanadu* and are high as kites.'

McHaffee smiled. He was not entirely sure if God was being stupid or unusually whimsical, or just star-struck by the famous rockers with the rhythmically memorable name.

'I'll try and get Vera Lynn if you'd prefer.'

'I'm forbidding all visitors for her until you get her bloody well sorted and out of here.'

So God had raged and raved on that encounter while smelling of whisky. Fine beads of sweat lined lined His brow.

In return McHaffee gave a smirk and shook his head.

That enraged God even more: 'I want you out, you little shit. Then we'll get a proper doctor in.'

McHaffee had a small degree of independent wealth and the sort of boldness which comes from a healthy bank account. The tirade left him unmoved. But he also had, in his jacket pocket, a photocopy of a letter he had received from his hero C.G. Jung, 10 years ago.

Jung had written, in reply to his youthful fan-mail which had been sent with 3 International Reply Coupons for return postage: '*The main interest of my work is not concerned with the treatment of neurosis but rather with the approach to the numinous, which is the real therapy.*' With that, McHaffee felt empowered to walk the endless, polished corridors of the wards like Christ in the Harrowing of Hell, bringing salvation to all, whether they deserved it or not.

To get Vicky 'sorted', as God had insisted, he really needed to find this Mr Grant.

Presently, via those lines of human contact that act like spirit paths across our inner landscapes, he found a person who knew a person who would make enquiries. And so he found himself in Golders Green knocking on Kenneth Grant's door at 11a.m. on the 11th day. The door opened slowly, as if for effect. The man before him wore a light summery suit with lemon shirt and spectacular tie. This was hardly the Gandalf or Saruman he had been warned about. Instead he faced a solidly-built middle-aged man with dark, swept-back and brylcreemed hair that framed a full face and a wry twinkling smile.

'Do what thou wilt shall be the whole of the Law,' said Mr. Grant.

'Hello,' said McHaffee, but not at all lamely.

He had been told to expect this greeting and advised as to the response: *Love is the Law: Love under Will*. But he was determined not to play this game and was making sure not to project onto his host either the role of Wise Old Man or Demon King.

Grant smiled and invited him in, then up to a book-lined room on the first floor where he placed him at a small table next to the window. While his host went to get tea McHaffee scanned the books. Apart from some fiction by HP Lovecraft, the rest covered arcane and obscure aspects of Eastern philosophies, none of which meant anything to him except that of Tantra. That was another concept which, in 1969, ranked alongside autism as the coming thing. There were numerous framed pictures on the walls, black and white heavily sexualised images of human and non-human creatures and scatterings of disturbing mandalas of a sort he had never seen used by Jung.

Grant returned carrying a small silver tray with a large red pot, milk and sugar and two small cups.

'Tell me about Babalon,' McHaffee asked, once the preliminaries had been dispensed with and tea sipped.

And so he listened and he tried to learn, but he found it hard to concentrate and Grant asked him – nicely – not to take notes. So the words became waves which broke on his mind and withdrew, leaving little bubbles which in themselves quickly popped. Babalon was a name for the Scarlet Woman, the Great Mother and – if you were scared of her – the Mother of Abominations. And if you weren't scared of her, she was also Mother Earth, who also guards the Abyss into which no sane person would want to fall.

'Does Babalon have a daughter? A Moonchild, perhaps?'

Then Grant opened a book by Crowley called *The Vision and the Voice*, to a description from the 9th Aethyr. He said that last as if everyone knew of the place and travelled into it regularly, like one the underground stations at Golders Green or Brent Cross..

'Crowley, the Seer, spoke of a child that has very deep eyelids and long lashes, and a body covered with fine gold hairs, like electric flames, and hair which flows down to her feet like a waterfall of light.'

That was nothing like Lilith, though it might have applied to her mother before the drugs wasted her. So he listened carefully – or tried to – because a small part of him wondered if Grant was trying to hypnotise him, his voice was so mellow and deep, rhythmic and compelling. His host then finished with:

'Crowley insisted that of all the glories he had witnessed in the Aethyrs, there was not one which was worthy to be compared with the daughter of Babalon's littlest finger-nail.'

McHaffee felt himself swaying in his chair. Had the tea been drugged? Crowley used to drug his guests, he had heard, in the days when even heroin was legal and cocaine was regularly prescribed by both Freud and Jung. *Hang on in there* he told himself and reached to his inside pocket for the photocopy of Jung's letter, as if it were the sacred bread of the Host. It must have looked as if he was reaching for a gun because Grant cocked his head, went silent and waited for the next question.

'Well, what about the actual Book of Babalon.'

Grant gave a laugh, rotated the strange rings on his hand so that they caught the afternoon light and reflected across the room like little comets. A tawny cat came in and jumped up on his lap, purring loudly.

'My familiar...Well, that book was 'received' as they say, in the American desert by a man called Jack Parsons. Now *he* was probably destined to become Crowley's heir if he hadn't blown himself up making rockets. Not the Guy Fawkes toys of Bonfire Night but big moon-going rockets. He was a pioneer in the field of rocket-propulsion. You know that NASA named an impact crater after him on the far side of the Moon?'

He didn't, of course he didn't, but he nodded anyway.

'Parsons felt that this *Book of Babalon,* more properly called *Liber 49*, was the fourth book of Crowley's *Book of the*

Law. Crowley himself never accepted that. And the old Beast rather lost faith when he and a man named Hubbard tried to create a Moonchild. Inspired by Crowley's novel of that name. They didn't create one in the physical plane but Parsons felt that he had opened gates for a new, feminine type of consciousness – Babalon – to eventually surge into and transform the world.'

'Not much evidence of that,' muttered McHaffee from the last weeks of 1969.

'Well this sort of thing can take a couple of generations. Have you read *Moonchild* by the way? It was originally called *The Butterfly Net.* A metaphor, of course, for the ritual used to catch an exalted soul. Here's a new edition. First one in 50 years. Keep it.'

McHaffee nodded thanks but he didn't want to open it or make the usual noises or promise he'd read every word.

'Time is,' said Grant looking at his watch. 'I must throw you out now. We've got a few wild witches coming around. Or would you like to stay?'

'No. I don't want to seem boring but I must go too. Thanks for your time.'

'Do you think you've met a Moonchild?'

'I've met someone who thinks they have. Personally I know she's just a little, troubled autistic girl.'

'Autistic eh? I heard someone mention that word only yesterday. I expect it will now become the Word of a very short Aeon among your tribe. But what is the little girl's first name? I'm not asking you to breach confidentiality here, but names have power, and significance.'

'Lilith.'

Grant beamed. 'You do know, I expect, that Lilith means 'Night Monster''?

'Yes,' he lied.

'You might want to go to the British Museum and see that terracotta plaque known as the Queen of the Night, from Old Babylon. Wonderfully sexy, deliciously disturbing.'

Then it seemed to his visitor as if Grant had a slight epileptiform 'absence' as he stared into the space behind him, seeing something on another level.

'Tell me mein doctor… is there anything odd about her feet? Oh my goodness I can see from your face that there is! Feet like bird claws, I'll wager! You've gone white. Would you like some water? Or an aspirin?'

'I must go.'

He rose and went down the stairs, holding the railing firmly. He felt as if his solar plexus had been ripped open and that spiritual guts were pouring out. At the door Grant thrust the novel *Moonchild* back into his hands and gave him a very earnest look.

'Listen Doctor McHaffee, *They* will come for her. Just as light will attract moths, what she might radiate will attract…well, I have confidentialities of my own calling that I mustn't breach. Unless you want to be responsible for cosmic storms and damnations and lose your very soul, then I'd advise you to run…'

The nearest tube station was Brent Cross with its entry columns like a Greek temple and its descent beyond them toward the underground.

McHaffee felt ill. He realised that he was not circling the plug hole but was actually spiralling down inside it. He walked unsteadily through the station, almost in curves. Anyone looking at him might have thought him drunk. He got on the first train which arrived and didn't care where it went. As it thundered and shook through those dark, sulphurous tunnels that laced beneath the city of London he put the book on the seat next to him and knew exactly what he had to do now: don't even open it, leave it where it is and get off at the next stop. The book itself would be carried on and down into the cthonic depths. At some point someone else would find it and become ensnared.

All he wanted to do now was get back across the river, shower, get clean on all sorts of levels, change his clothes and wash Vicky and Lilith from his life as quickly as he could.

One of Lilith's most precious possessions, and one that she would keep until the end of her life, was a small, silver-rimmed two-sided mirror from the empty budgie cage. The sort that was supposed to fool the bird into thinking it had company.

She removed the mirror and kept it close, always hidden, because she realised that if she looked at it in the dark then Sister Endlove would appear as a greater darkness, solid and cuddly, warm and kind.

She did so that night and sighed as the space around her bed became dusky and wrapped itself around, and the familiar arms encircled her.

'Your shadow is very deep tonight,' said Lilith.

'That's because, from somewhere, I'm getting a whole lot of light.'

'Hug me again. Please.'

So she was hugged, and sank into the comfort as if it might be the last.

'You know that I will not come to this place again.' said Endlove with a voice that was so much like a calm sea.

Lilith gave a tiny nod. Somehow she knew that. Perhaps it was the far side of the Moon which told her such things.

'Will I be safe?'

'You will be be *very* safe. Someone is coming.'

'Will I be taken from here?'

'Oh yes. Far from here.'

'Will I lose my Mummy? She's the best Mummy in the world.'

'No-one ever loses their Mummy. They are always here,' she said, touching Lilith's chest. 'In different ways and places and times.'

'What about the other children here?'

'They must stay.'

'Poor things.'

'They were cruel to you.'

'Yes.'

'Very cruel.'

'Yes.'

'You could say goodbye to them now, in your own very special way.'

Lilith thought hard, looking out at the sleeping children in the dorm. And then she looked into the little mirror, turning one side and then the next, angling it to see into the night. Sometimes, when she did this, she felt very old and got all sorts of ideas.

What would Mummy say?

What would Mummy do?

'Ba Ba Babalon...' she whispered.

'Nighty-night Lilith,' said Sister Ndlovu as the girl got off the bed and tiptoed toward Wayne.

Lilith went to the other children one by one. With that hidden side of her that no-one had seen she sliced and spliced into their dreams. She did things to them, gliding through their night, that would make sure they would never be hurtful to her again, never sneer, spit in her food, throw things or laugh at her feet and the way she walked.

'Time is,' she said to the house then stretched out on her bed and slept.

Thou shalt offer all thou art and all thou hast at my altar, withholding nothing. And thou shalt be smitten full sore and thereafter thou shalt be outcast and accursed, a lonely wanderer in abominable places.

The Book of Babalon

While Lilith was wrapped in the night of Sister Endlove, McHaffee had a dream. He had gone to bed sorely troubled by his meeting with Grant without being able to say why. He knew even while it was going on that this was a Big Dream. Of the sort that Jung had written about in his *Memories Dreams and Reflections*. In this lucid Big Dream he was at the sea shore, on a paradisical island. Neatly dressed as if for work but wearing Nurse Hawkins' socks without shoes. There was no sun but a snow-white moon in a pale blue sky and a man on his left side, slightly behind, dressed like a kingfisher.

The violet waves before him withdrew. This was not done slowly and subtly, with the push and pull of a normal tide building up its retreat. Instead they pulled back quickly, like a conjurer whipping away a table cloth and leaving the cups in place.

He didn't question this; he followed the retreating waters. The Kingfisher Man, who looked a bit like his own father, put a hand out to stop him but he pushed it away.

The beach underfoot was wonderful, bare and flat and silvery-white sand. All manner of things were revealed when the waters withdrew: anchors, sunken boats, goblets, treasures, human bones. He felt privileged to look upon things no-one had seen before. Further out still a shoal of large salmon flapped and gasped and gave him their last knowing looks on the sand. Some of them were rotting and their shiny bodies gave off that smell he always associated with sex.

My my my... he said as the waters continued to pull back and blend with the distant horizon. The air was unnaturally calm. He could hear his own heart-beat.

Then there was a whisper in his left ear, perhaps from the White Moon itself who seemed to using all its power to attract the waters:

The tsunami is coming...

McHaffee felt terror. He turned to run, knowing that he had to find higher ground. Behind him, roaring, coming closer by the second, he knew that a mighty wave was on its way...

A light blazed out from somewhere, turning Nurse Hawkins' spiky blonde hair into a cartoon sun, looming in his face. A cool, small hand touched his brow. Another on his chest.

'Do you often have nightmares?' she asked, pulling the blankets around him. 'You've never been the same since you bought that nasty book.. You look like a frightened little boy.'

'I am. Don't know why. I'm out of my depth. I feel as if I'm drowning'

'I quite like you drowning like this!'

'Later today I'll have one last meeting with a client and then I think we should...should...oh I don't know. Anything healthy, anything normal.'

'Go skydiving? Yes? YES! I knew I'd get you to lighten up. Come here and let me rescue you...'

Come morning, at work, McHaffee shredded his copy of the *Book of Babalon* and disposed of the bits downstairs. Then he returned to his office and waited for Vicky, summoning up what to say and how to drop her from his care in a way that wouldn't send her over the edge. She turned up very late for her appointment. The new digital clock showed the time as exactly 13.13. McHaffee rather dreaded this moment but in the event *she* dropped *him.*

'You're fired,' she said brightly, springing into the room and closing the door after her. Her hair had been washed, some discreet make-up applied. She was still wasted, still jaundiced, but she was wearing a floaty blue designer dress that came down to her calves and a white jacket with sleeves that covered her needle marks. 'I'm better now, see, I told you. Just needed some antibiotics.'

On a normal day he would disagree. On *this* day, after *that* nightmare, he said nothing. This was his way of finding higher ground and avoiding whatever tsunami might be coming.

'Thank you for sharing that.'

'But my dear, dear Doctor Kildare – or is it Doctor Finlay? – or Dr Doolittle? Anyway I mean, I've been discharged. God loves me.'

Do you mean God in Heaven or the Physician Superintendent upstairs?

'Both, I suppose. And God really doesn't like *you.*'

'Do you mean the Physician Superintendent upstairs or God in Heaven?'

'Both. I've had long talks with each. Anyway, here's my discharge papers to prove it.'

He looked at them. They proved it. He tried to maintain a professional mask and not show relief.

'So where will you go?'

'Keef and Anita are coming to get me.'

He had no idea who they were and didn't want to find out. He just wanted higher ground, clearer ground. The simple sunniness of Nurse Hawkins would help him.

'What about Lilith?

'What about her?'

'Don't you care about her?'

She frowned. A cheerful mock frown.

'Erm...no. I didn't ask for her to be born. I didn't ask for a *Mooon*child.'

'What about the father? Can I ask who he was? If you know, that is.'

'Ooh, chee-*kyyy*... We had a one-night stand on a barge on the Regent's Canal. But what a night, and what a stand! I was only 16. We were probably the first people in the country to take LSD. I was his first. Next day he hadn't a clue.'

'Who is he?'

'Name of Kaspar, I think. He's a cripple. A spastic. But then again the Child Horus had bad legs too. He kept chanting *Ba Ba Babalon* while we did it. I think. Anyway, afterwards, on the tube, I found the *Book of Babalon* that someone had just left. It called to me. It was even better than *Jonathan Livingston Seagull*. I knew it was all about me and *for* me.'

'Did you ever meet Kenneth Grant?'

'Dear old Aossic? That would be telling! I owe everything to military-strength acid and that one night with the weirdo Kaspar. He's probably from beyond the Sun. Mars maybe. No idea where he is now and I don't care, my luvvy. Probably on the Mothership. He's probably got the best Mothership in the Galaxy.'

On *another* normal day McHaffee would have risen to the challenge Vicky offered (or was it bait?). After all Jung himself had written about Flying Saucers, defining them as a modern myth. To him, aliens must be perceived and understood in terms of human symbolic systems. Today though, he had had enough.

'Are you just going to abandon Lilith?

'Listen you loony, she's a *Mooon*child. Her sort are never abandoned. Someone is coming for her, someone so powerful and terrifying and irresistible that nothing is going to stand in the way. Me, I've got a life to live from now on and never want to see the little freak again. I'm gonna surf on out of here hanging five when that wave of yours arrives. Bye Bye *Bye-Bye-Bye* you funny little man...'

The Matron was not having a good morning. It was raining heavily outside and she had left her washing out. And there was also a funny atmosphere about the Home when she arrived. The children ate their breakfasts quietly instead of whining and making pathetic attempts to get attention. Her staff, never warm toward her at best, seemed awkward and kept out of her way. So when she heard the doorbell ring ring and not stop ringing she flounced out of her office ready to draw blood.

On the doorstep was a hefty lady whose clothes, if not her person, smelled of damp earth She wore an old, light brown 3/4 length coat made of drill material, over a pair of equally old dungarees. The smell of damp earth came from the mud on her boots as if she had just come from the local Farmers' Market. Her greying hair exploded from under a battered wide-brimmed felt hat.

'I thought the Women's Land Army disbanded after the war,' said The Matron, feeling rather pleased at own wit.

'I've come for Lilith,' said the visitor brusquely and made to push past.

The Matron stood her ground and blocked the door.

'Here's my authorisation,' said the interloper, handing her a sheaf of documents.

The Matron frowned, scanned the documents, shook her head, determined to let this idiot stand out in the rain.

'This shows nothing. Proves nothing. Lilith is under my care and she will not be removed from here unless I get written approval from the very highest source.'

'Such as?'

'Well, the Director of Social Services for a start.'

'I can get higher than that,' said the visitor. 'I'll be back in an hour.'

The Matron watched her climb into her Land Rover Defender and drive off, burning oil.

'Who was that?' asked the Deputy Matron coming up behind.

'Some nutter. I gave her what for. Won't see her again.'

'Matron...'

'What?'

'I need to talk to you about Lilith and the others. Something very odd has happened.'

One hour later The Matron answered the door to *two* women this time, the second one protecting her lavishly permed fair hair under a small umbrella. She was about to slam the door in their face but recognised the other and went pale. The Land Woman - she could hardly be called a Land *Girl* at her age - beamed.

'You know my oldest and best friend Violet, don't you Matron? Everyone in this manor knows *you*, don't they Vi?'

'Oh shush, you'll make me blush. I remember when matron here was just Batty Brenda. You went to school with my twin boys in Daniel Street. You remember me, don't you Brenda? You know who I am?'

Brenda the Matron knew exactly who she was. Her twin sons Reg and Ron were gangsters. They ruled North London and they adored their mum, the best mum in the world as they were often heard to say. No-one would dare disagree.

'Yes, Mrs Kray.'

'Let's go in out of the rain...'

The Matron ushered them into the small office with an olive-green door. She wasn't exactly bowing and scraping but there was only a hairs-breadth in it. The door was closed. The Matron sat behind her desk, if only to hide the shaking of her knees. All the nursing qualifications in the world, all the power and status of the uniform and its badges wouldn't protect her. And none of the bent coppers, dodgy magistrates or corrupted Justices of the Peace would come near her now because of that cheery woman's sons. The Land Woman was right: she had summoned a far higher authority in this area than any poxy Director of Social Services. This was London

49

in the Swinging Sixties when men were men – and did exactly as their mothers told them.

'This place looks run down Brenda. I see that naughty Tom Driberg has been donating his old rubbish. Watch out for him, mind. Him and my Ron were very good friends for a time. Shall I send someone to sort things out? No? You sure? One of our pals, Frankie Fraser, loves a bit of DIY.'

'Is that the one they call *Mad* Frankie Fraser?' asked the Land Woman, delighting in the moment. 'The one with the axe?'

'No you silly mare, that's Frank Mitchell. *He* fell out with our Reg but he seems to have disappeared off the face of the earth.'

'Listen...' muttered the Matron.

'No, *you* listen Brenda. I've got a lot of stuff on you but hey – live and let live is my motto. Just sign these papers and we'll collect little Lilith and we'll be out of your life forever. Deal?'

She signed, with shaking hand. When the two older women left the office they could hear it being locked behind them.

The other staff recognised Mrs Kray too. They stood aside as she swept into the lounge.

'Where is this Lilith then?' she asked the Deputy Matron.

'There. They're all sitting in a group watching *Mary, Mungo and Midge*. Only thing is, it's not even on today but they're all glued to it. And glued to Lilith.'

In fact they were sitting around her, at her feet, like little lion cubs. The mood was warm and protective. In their own ways, their faces shone.

'Look at Wayne,' whispered the Deputy Matron, looking with wonder. 'The biggest boy. Last night he had the most dreadful warts on his face, now they're gone. Isn't he handsome now! And Maggie - Maggie had eczema. And Janet had stress-related psoriasis and the others all have -'

'Shush,' said the Land Woman. 'I get the picture. This is my moment.'

'Hello Lilith,' she said, kneeling before her, blocking the picture on the telly. The girl didn't seem to mind. 'You don't know me but I've been trying to find you for a long time. I've come to take you away.'

'Have you come from Mummy?'

'Well, sort of. She wants me to take care of you now. I will get you some nice clothes, and special shoes for these funny little feet and we'll live in a pretty valley where you'll have a goat and owls and you'll make lots of friends.'

'Will I get a dog?'

'If you want.'

And a mouse?

'Settle for a hamster. Same thing. Come, give me cuddle.'

The Land Woman stood up, cuddling her, and walked to the door. The other children grouped around and touched the hem of Lilith's nightie that she was still wearing. All of them said quiet *thank yous*, for secret things done in the middle of the night, at the edges of their sleep, making their rotten lives just a bit easier for them in ways that only they knew.

Wayne came up and he drew from behind his back the butterfly net that he had fixed for her with lashings of tape.

'Sorry. Can we be friends now?'

'No.'

The Land Woman put Lilith on the front seat of her car, on a cushion, wrapped in a blanket. Then she put the seat-belt around her saying: 'Clunk-Click Every Trip!' echoing the campaign fronted by that jolly philanthropist Jimmy Savile, in the 50 years before the world found out that he was pure evil. Lilith held the butterfly net in one hand and the budgie mirror in the other. Her eyes were huge. She shook a little.

'Who are you?'

The big old woman smelled of earth. She had a box full of apples in the back seats. Her large round full-moony face was fringed with grey hair poking wildly from her hat. She gave Lilith the biggest and happiest and safest of smiles.

'I'm your Granny. And I'm going to be the best Granny in the world...'

Lilith came to realise, over the years, that being a Moonchild was easy. All she needed to do was be very still and reflect light from other sources. It was easy but also painful. The Moon itself was shaped by the impact of cosmic rubbish smashing into its face. Unlike the Earth, the Moon has no atmosphere to protect itself. And Lilith's mother, lacking just such an atmosphere, would one day become as cratered and as dead, waxing and waning only in her daughter's memories. If Granny hadn't come for Lilith when she did then even a *Mooon*child would have become no more than a casualty of her era: labelled as autistic, schizophrenic and crippled; shut away and ignored. When Lilith grew up she would hear a lot of people talking a lot of nonsense about Saviours, but she came to realise that in her life there had only ever been one, and that was Granny.

Our souls all go 'into the West' when we die, usually in a state of bliss. But the last time Granny had actually driven there from London was during the war, when her part of the city became Doodlebug Alley. Every day the civilians watched the black rocket-powered crucifixes of the V1 flying bombs pulsing overhead. The only rule of survival was to dive for cover as soon as the throbbing stopped.

She was only 20 then and doing her bit on nearby farms with the Women's Land Army, replacing the men who had been called up to fight. Fearing for her parents' lives, she had hijacked an old lorry and drove them and all their meagre possessions toward distant relatives. Before setting off, though, she had even offered to make a second trip for her neighbour Violet Kray, who was struggling with her children, and whose husband had gone into hiding to avoid conscription.

'You're a star you are,' said Violet, with teary eyes. 'An absolute star. But no thanks, luv, I'll live and die here where I belong. Besides, my Charlie might come back any day. Listen, if there's ever anything I can do for you, *ever,* I won't let you down...'

Nor did she. Granny was pleased that her random acts of kindness over the years, done without apparent need or purpose, seemed to have spread like the rhizomes of plants, breaking the surface of her life at unexpected moments and giving rewards of strange fruit.

Now, with Lilith snoring in the front seat, still clutching the butterfly net and budgie mirror, Granny was heading to the cottage in a deep valley on the border between Wiltshire and Somerset that, in her mind, represented safety and salvation.

The house lay halfway down the sides of the valley. Granny approached it by a narrow road that curved between grey, drystone walls, bending right and then sharply down, giving way to a mini-hairpin bend that she could do in one if she got her angles exact. Her foot was on the squealing brake, the Defender trailing clouds of stinking oil. The whole valley, as far across as Freshford, could probably hear them coming.

Ssh Ssh she said to the car.

She parked in a small cutting at the side of the road, just above the house. She was relieved to see the lights were on and that her friends were waiting.

'Dicky Bird House', she whispered to Lilith when they arrived. 'We're here. One hour of daylight left at this level. See how the valley below is already filled with night.'

Lilith never stirred.

At the bottom of the descending path, three women emerged from the cottage. One of them crunched all the way up to the car and helped Granny lift the mite from the seat. It was awkward because Lilith still gripped the butterfly net and mirror in her sleep. They closed the car door silently as if there was more need for secrecy than fear of waking the child.

'She's here at last,' the helper whispered, looking with wonder at the little white-faced bundle curved into Granny's arms.

Half way down the path Granny managed to slide the pole of the net from Lilith's fingers and pushed it down into the earth where it remained, fluttering in the breeze like a wind sock.

A second woman, very smiley, almost danced on the balls of her feet when she glimpsed the child. 'I do believe you've done it!" she also whispered. 'Oh you star! I always knew this would happen.'

'Shush,' said Granny pushing past and into the cottage. There, two table lamps at either side of the small room provided a soft light. A fire burned in the hearth tended by the third woman who just looked with sheeny eyes, holding both hands up in a kind of salute, showing that all her fingers were crossed.

Of course Lilith had been awake for a couple of hours but feigned sleep. She had never been in a car before; the rhythm and warmth and smell of apples from the back seat kept her dozing, never quite falling back into true sleep. Cozy and safe at last. When they stopped she felt the cool air of her face as she was carried down a path, allowed Granny to remove the butterfly net and still pretended when she was carried into the amber jewel of the room.

She was aware of being lowered onto what must have been a couch, where she could stretch out. She was aware of being looked at. She was aware that there was a very different tone to *their* scrutiny. When living with Mummy the visitors, when they even noticed her, had peered down and said – or thought – *Ugh.* Sometimes she heard them saying cruel things, often laughing. Mummy never once stood up for her other than saying – though not always – *She's a Mooonchild.*

Here, under a soft light at the other side of her tightly closed eyelids she heard:

I've got my tape measure. I'll measure her funny little feet and get some special shoes made.

I'll go into Bath tomorrow and get her a complete set of day clothes and night clothes.

I'll get her some kiddies books and toys. I bet she'd love a tricycle.

Lilith frowned but kept her eyes closed. With the far side of her soul that no-one saw, she had experienced all kinds of things: simple kindness was unknown. For the first time in the endless, dreadful and neglected moments of her short life she began to formulate the thinnest sliver of a notion: perhaps her Mummy *wasn't* the best Mummy in the world. Then she stopped that thought completely, as all small children do, as a revelation too much

Sssh, said Granny, *she's stirring.*

Unable to resist, Lilith opened her eyes once. She knew they wanted this. She knew that there was something about her eyes that scared people, but…

The three women, all of them with wild hair or hats, gasped, but instead of drawing back in revulsion as everyone else had done, these lot were drawn forward, as if they wanted to cuddle her. Lilith closed her eyes again and pretended to drop back off to sleep. Their gasps were not disgust, not fear, not hatred. Their faces all seemed so *happy.* No-one that Lilith had met had ever been happy to see her. This was something else she would have to learn.

The one who had waited at the bottom of the path, with flame-red fluffy hair and piercing blue eyes, was almost dancing with delight. She couldn't resist bursting into a whispered song:

'I know that my Redeemer liveth, and that *She* shall stand at the latter day upon the earth. And though worms destroy this body, yet in my flesh shall I see...'

'Oh shut up, Hope.'

'But that's adapted from Handel's Messiah!'

'I don't care if its from the Bonzo Dog Doo-Dah Band, you're always off-key. Just don't sing.'

So she didn't, yet although she didn't move a muscle it was obvious she was dancing a jig.

'I hope you'll be able to manage,' said the second.

'I will. Don't you worry. I'm told she's got something called sleep-wake inversion. If so it's going to be a long night for me tonight. And I don't want her getting confused by all you old biddies. I've got to bond with my lovely little grand-daughter.'

'We'd better go,' said the third. 'We're on a mission now aren't we girls? I do love shopping.'

'Bye bye Granny!' they all said in leaving.

Lilith could feel the swirlings of the warm air as they left, but not before each one touched her gently, very gently. She could feel them glowing though she didn't know why. With her excellent hearing she heard the three of them whisper:

This time.

This one.

Now it begins.

The front door opened and closed, quietly, and she heard them tiptoeing up the stony path and the sound of something outside that she would soon learn was called Owl. Her plan was to keep her eyes closed for a little while longer until night properly fell, then she would see her new world.

Well, she might have been a Moonchild whose soul had been summoned from the absolute nothingness of interstellar space, and received her visits from the Three Wise Women, *and* be in the process of fulfilling ancient, secret prophecies. But all she could think about was getting a tricycle.

'They're gone now Lilith,' said Granny. 'I know you're not asleep.'

Lilith opened her eyes.

'They all called you Granny. How can you be *their* Granny?'

'Well actually my name is really Gráinne - *Graw nya* – which sounds a lot like Granny don't you think? But they call me Granny like a kind tease. They're all a bit jealous because I've got you. I call *them* Faith, Hope and Charity. That's not their real names, but it's a kind of a joke among us. Nothing to do with the Bible.'

Lilith frowned. She didn't know what the Bible was.

'Just know, little girl, that we're all so glad you've come to live with us. Forever and forever. What do you think of that?'

'Time is,' she said, using the habitual response.

'Stuff and nonsense. You don't need to say things from that stupid book any more. Stuff. And. Nonsense.'

That was another revelation. She stored those three words into the far side of her mind to deal with later.

'Mummy always told me that I'm a Moonchild.'

'You are certainly that, Lilith, and one day you'll be the best *Moon*child that ever there was, or will be. But you've got to learn to be an *Earth*child first because one can't exist without the other. That's why I'm here...'

'But can I have a dog? And a mouse? And a tricycle?'

'Oh you and me are going to be such good friends...'

When Lilith was much older she would look back upon Dicky Bird House as a living thing. Instead of flesh it had old, honeyed stone; instead of bones it had the walls of two bedrooms, a small sitting room, a narrow kitchen and a cold bathroom made of breeze blocks tagged on at the end; instead of blood it had electricity, accessed by the old round-pin plugs that were already obsolete. The body heat came from the single coal fire.

It was old and run-down but embraced her every much as Sister Ndlovu and Granny. Fifty years before, it had been known as the Gardener's Cottage, on the very edge of a large manor but overlooked by no-one. With the far side of her mind, tilting and twisting the little mirror to help, she knew that the last gardener had left because his wife and only child had died in the upstairs room while giving birth.

This tragedy caused Lilith no torment. The people in the mirror seemed to tell her that by being here with Granny she was – somehow – making it up for them.

'Let's have a look around your new home shall we?'

Lilith nodded. That was another new concept. *Mary Mungo and Midge* had a home. She wasn't sure if she was allowed.

Her bare feet almost gave individual gasps when she stood on the thick green, wall-to-wall carpet and she wasn't shy of showing Granny her claw-like toes. The walls were papered with ridiculous, large sunflowers though the joins were not all perfectly matched, as it had been Granny's first attempt.

At the end of the sitting room, opposite a small but empty bookcase was what Lilith thought was a cupboard door. Instead it opened to a higgledy staircase that led into Granny's own room with its big bed, two creaky old wardrobes, a sideboard and full length mirror. And the door at the side of that room led to:

'This is *your* room, Lilith.'

Peeking in, shyly, she marvelled at the Big Girl's bed which was not a cot-cum-cage. It had bright red covers and fluffy pillows with lace edges and a hot water-bottle shaped like a teddy bear and a little plastic potty.

Best of all there was a window at the very end that she immediately peered out of, onto the garden, and saw the butterfly net sighing in the wind and glistening with light from the rising moon.

'Get this old rubbish off you and wrap yourself in this big towel. I'm going to run you a bath now and then we'll get you into a *new* nightie and posh dressing gown. And then I'll read you stories while you drink warm milk and honey.'

Lilith didn't know what to say. Granny pulled a face.

'Lilith, what you must learn to say when someone – anyone – does something nice and kind to you, is *Thank You.* Can you say that? Louder please! At my age I'm a little deaf. Oh good. Very good.'

Granny finished filling the bath, whipped up the bubbles then tested the water with her elbow and went into the sitting room. The towel lay on the floor. No sign of her granddaughter. With a rising sense of fear she clattered up the wooden staircase, catching her feet on the awkward turn and found both rooms empty.

'And *breathe...*' she told herself to control her panic. She couldn't call her friends for help as there was no phone. This was 1969 and few people in Britain had one.

It was the open curtains and the radiance beyond that stopped her screaming out Lilith's name. There, with her delicate feet trampling the soft grass of the unkempt little lawn, was a naked little girl dancing in the moonlight. One side of her was white-silver, the other purpley-black, interchanging as she turned, arms raised to the sky. She might have been singing, but with the window closed and her own poor hearing Granny couldn't be sure. Yet whatever song was flowing through her bent little body was surely a happy one.

Lilith stopped when she heard the *hoo hoo hoooo* of Owl and the bleating of Goat in the field below. Then she saw that she was being watched from the window. Had she done wrong? No...Granny's big round face was happy and was giving her a thumbs up with both hands.

'Lilith,' she said, coming out to the garden to wrap her in the towel again. 'Let's get you into the bath before it gets cold.'

'Thank you. Thank you...*Granny*,' she whispered, and didn't understand why the big, warm old lady made a noise like a sob and kept her face turned away. But at least she knew she hadn't been naughty.

Granny came to realise very quickly that raising a Moonchild was not easy. She had to learn what sort of light to shine on this unformed little girl and from what angle and how intensely, lest it create even more impact craters. She spent the first 48 hours in a state of exhaustion and eventually had to speak to Lilith's 'other' side, hoping it would hear: *I need you to sleep at night and be awake during the day. Can you turn it around, please?* And on the third day Lilith emerged from the night and stayed wide-awake all day. *Thank you*, said Granny, aware that a revolution had occurred.

So it was hard but also wonderful.

Yet Granny was more than just an elderly lady doing her best. When Slicky Vicky had ranted to McHaffee she pulled aside a curtain leading to Mysteries. Granny, too, was one of the intra-class, for lack of a better term: existing quietly in the cracks and fissures of society, being lubricant and glue, holding worlds together. She was earthbound and also star-born, though few would ever realise judging from her working boots and dungarees and old Land Army greatcoat. This intra-class was always female, acting quietly, without fuss, without display, without becoming purple-wearing crystal-bearing maxim-spouting, self-styling and money-hungry Adeptii desperate for the front pages. Or, these days, via blogs and vlogs and little videos on the internet.

Granny was the real thing and Granny was near invisible.

She aimed to teach Lilith, when she was still young and likely to listen: *Be aware that the little old whiskery lady in the corner, with her funny hat and tea and Victoria Sponge cake, is likely to be a very special soul. Be nice.*

She thought Lilith's little budgie mirror was an item of genius, as she saw her glancing into it whenever she was puzzled. Granny never challenged. She knew from the ancient Jewish myths about her granddaughter's name-sake that every mirror is a gateway to the Other World and leads directly to Lilith's cave.

What did Jewish myths know though! *Her* Lilith, thrilled with her new shoes that supported her feet and ankles but also hid her bird-like toes, was a *very* different being.

So Granny herself was also something of a Moonchild, as were her friends Faith, Hope and Charity - as were *all* women if they knew how and where to look inside. It was never a question of belonging to sacred bloodlines or secret groups and Orders: the Mystery was there, on the far side of everyone's Moon, if they could only learn to twist around and see it. Faith worked as a cleaner in posh peoples' homes in the Limpley Stoke valley; Hope as a nursing auxiliary in the Winsley Chest Hospital; Charity – or Chazza as she liked to be called because she was a Cockney – ran an Oxfam shop in Bath which still exists, although she has long since been forgotten.

No-one knew what flowed through and between them, or how they influenced realms.

'They are Peacock butterflies,' she said to Lilith, seeing her at the far side of the garden, beyond the potato patch. The girl was absorbed by a small tree which was completely covered in the red and black creatures. 'Those markings on the wings look like eyes to scare off mice. I think they're all here to say hello to you.'

'Hello. Shall I catch them with my net?'

'No, never! The net has done its job in catching you and bringing you here.'

The tree throbbed like a vein, with the mass of fluttering wings and the flashing eyes. Lilith put her face very close. She could feel the pulsing air.

'What do you see?'

Lilith looked closely with her left eye and then the right.

'People,' she whispered.

'They're all the souls we didn't manage to catch over the years.'

'Are they happy?'

'They are now.'

A part of Lilith, still waiting for her tricycle, didn't understand. Another part understood completely, though she couldn't have voiced it. The side of Lilith that was from beyond the stars never had to put *everything* into words.

'But lovey, look what I've made for you!'

She gave Lilith a silver chain with a clasp on the end that would fasten onto the little round mirror and showed her how to wear it around her neck like a medal.

'Thank you.'

'Now come and see Goat...'

Lilith liked Goat. It had the strangest eyes. The horizontal pupils seemed to see all around with moving, without needing a mirror to make sense of things. It nuzzled her. And it had feet likes hers, sort of, only with two toes instead of three.

'Goat uses its mouth to touch and feel, just like we do with our hands.'

It put its mouth to her mirror.

'It won't eat it! Don't let that daft Chazza warn about Goat eating tin cans and things. It doesn't. Just don't let it out and near our shrubs and vegetables because then she really will eat everything. She gives us our milk.'

'Thank you.'

She liked Goat so much that she was going to call it Mungo and was not going to ask for a dog any more. Truth is, Lilith had noticed that when she last mentioned that to Granny, the woman had a sharp intake of breath and stared into the middle distance. Lilith didn't need her budgie mirror to guess what she was thinking then: *Could she cope with a*

Moonchild and a flamin' dog? So she pretended to forget that little wish. Lilith didn't know much about the ways of the world but she was innately kind. That would one day be her salvation, although it wouldn't come easily.

'Here, try this for size,' said Granny, lifting her up and put her astride Goat. 'Hold onto the little horns.'

Goat seemed quite happy with this; Lilith was so small and light it didn't trouble her. In fact it ambled across the field to where Granny had left some hay, its rider almost shining.

'Oh I wish I had a camera!' squealed Granny. 'Who needs a pony, eh?'

As the beast buried its face into the hay, Lilith caught a glimpse of someone hiding in the bushes beyond.

'Who is that little boy, Granny?'

Granny froze. She followed the pointing finger but saw nothing. Then she grabbed Lilith by the waist and hurried her back into the house like a sack of potatoes, plumped her down on the couch below the level of the window, peering out through the net curtains on that side.

'What did you see?'

'A little boy.'

'What did he look like?'

'Don't know.'

'What was he wearing?'

'White. Something white. He was smiling but I think he was sad. Can we go back to Goat again?'

'No. No, I'm going to read you stories for a while. You need some proper stories – real stories.'

Lilith didn't know what that meant. The only book that Mummy had ever read to her was the *Book of Babalon*. She had done so in a loud voice, often from the far side of the room and in company with nasty people. Lilith knew the words but had no understanding. And sometimes, it seemed to her, Mummy didn't either. Once she had thrown the book down saying: *It needs rewriting. that's your job, Lilith. One day.* All Lilith could think of in reply was: *Time is, Mummy –* which got her a wry laugh.

Granny grabbed a few of the books that Chaz had brought and hauled Lilith onto her lap, but kept looking outside. It took three whole stories before Lilith felt her Granny calm down. She didn't have the skills to ask her *why* she was worried, or frightened by the boy. She had only seen him for a second, but she liked him. This boy was nothing like Wayne.

Those *real* stories of Granny's were by a woman called Enid Blyton and the first two books were: *The Adventures of the Wishing Chair* and *The Enchanted Wood*.

'Choose…'

Lilith pointed at the latter. She curved and curled into Granny and found that she fitted even better than with Sister Ndlovu. As Granny's voice took on a deep tone she listened with the sort of rapture that Mummy seemed to have when mainlining. She learned how Joe, Beth and Frannie moved to a new home with an Enchanted Wood on their doorstep which had a Faraway Tree that could take them to the Land of Spells, the Land of Treats, or the Land of Do-As-You-Please. And they had new friends there in Moonface, Saucepan Man and Silky the fairy.

Granny read the whole book, doing all the different voices, doing the Talking in Tongues that makes things come alive. She looked out of the window a final time and shrugged, relaxing completely.

'It doesn't come better than this, does it?' she asked of the tiny dark-eyed wide-eyed girl with a thumb in her mouth, not needing an answer.

'I think it was Silky the fairy I saw outside.'

'I expect it was. But nothing and no-one can get past Granny…'

Thou shalt prepare my book for her instruction, also thou shalt teach that she may have captains and adepts in her service. Yea, thou shalt take the black pilgrimage, but it will not be thou that returnest.

The Book of Babalon

And Lilith liked Owl. It also had feet like hers, but more spread out. Granny told her that owls don't really sleep all day and wake all night to go hunting, any more than goats will eat tin cans. But nor did Lilith really sleep all night as Granny had supposed. She didn't need much sleep at all, and besides everything in her new world was an adventure, better than anything Joe, Frannie and Beth had.

Every night she would wait until she heard Granny snoring in the next room and creep to the end of her bed to look out of the window. Ordinary folk might see only variations of darkness, broken only by the distant necklaces of light from houses along the valley: Lilith never saw darkness. For Lilith, night was always filled with moonlight leaking into every nook and cranny whether the real thing was risen or not. She knew that the Moon was out there somewhere – wherever it was she could always feel it. As the wind in the trees made a sound like the sea, she saw the valley as surging waves of the astral light, filled with strange creatures that Granny would always protect her from.

She could see Owl on his tree now, clear as anything. And earlier that day she had seen Snake slithering through the grass right toward Chazza who had screamed, and Faith said it might be a poisonous adder, and Hope had jumped onto a low wall but Granny said it was only a harmless grass snake, silly mares. Lilith didn't know what any of these were, but she sort of told it to stop and did, right in front of her, and gave a look and slithered away toward the willow tree.

'See,' said Granny in a meaningful voice, and they all went in for tea while Lilith played with Goat again.

Lilith was starting to learn about meaningful voices by listening to all the stories. The flat cartoons of *Mary, Mungo and Midge* had taken her as far they could in terms of explaining the world: *The Enchanted Wood* and the *Faraway Tree,* no matter how silly they might seem, were opening her awareness.

All adults keep a little child prisoner within them. When they head toward their deaths they engage with that mite again and again, in different ways. Yet some adults, no matter how old they get, never evolve beyond being a 14 year old, and these are the ones who damage everyone that comes close.

No matter how old Granny was when she read the stories, she never wanted them to end any more than Lilith did, because they put her in touch with lost things.

And no matter how young Lilith was when she listened to them, there was a very old Person hiding within that needed such yarns to learn how this new world in which she found herself worked.

Lilith was outside with a trowel digging up some weeds between the carrots, wearing girl-sized dungarees to be like Granny. Inside, two big people were watching.

'She's not wearing the shoes I bought her,' said Faith, who had popped in after doing some cleaning at the nearby manor. They both peered out through the net curtains which allowed them to see without being seen.'

'Oh she loves them, but seems to prefer being barefoot when she's outside here, and dashes back to put them if the postie or paperboy come down the path. Disguise. You should say the way she can climb the tree to see Owl.'

'How is she getting on?'

Granny considered. She did that by pressing her lips together hard and squeezing her hands together rather like Lilith did.

'As far as little girls go, she is behind for her years. But that's to be expected, considering her time with Victoria. So I pump into her all the very young stories and sit down with her in front of the telly that Chazza brought, and she hoovers it all up.'

'But…?'

'Then there are the times when I know I'm sharing space and time with a very very very *very* old *Thing* who is rather indulging me, but we all expected that.'

'Thing is an odd word.'

'I don't mean it nastily. Not like those little shits in the orphanage or Victoria's useless hangers on. But we all know that what lies behind the little girl is not exactly…well, human.'

'Human plus, Gráinne .'

'Yes, of course. But listen Faith, do you know if any of the families around here have a little boy? I mean in the manor, particularly?'

'Yes, a number of them do. You worried about the one she saw?'

'No, I suppose not. I'm sure it really was just a boy. Lilith didn't seem afraid. I think she'd have gone across the stream to play if I hadn't grabbed her. Anyway, you won't believe the stuff that little mite can do…'

'Like the telly…'

Chazza had recently brought them a small, white plastic black and white portable television with a loop aerial. She carried it into Dicky Bird House as though it was a holy object, and wore her usual look of insufferable smugness, one eyebrow seemingly always raised to the idiocies of the modern world. She worked in a charity shop in Bath but as a young woman had been dropped into Occupied France and later Holland as a member of the Special Operations Executive.

'Thanks Chazza, but we won't get a signal here, down in the valley,' Granny had said. 'I tried that years ago.'

Nevertheless she plugged it in, put it on a small table between the fireplace and the window and switched it on. Nothing more than a fuzz of rolling lines and electronic sounds no matter how much she twisted and turned the aerial.

Lilith came down from upstairs, still in her nightie, touched the aerial and the picture burst onto the screen, crystal clear, perfect sound. Without a word she sat down in front of it and watched *The Clangers,* about a family of creatures who live on, and inside, a small moon-like planet. They spoke only in whistles, and ate only green soup that was supplied by the Soup Dragon, and finished their meals with blue string pudding. And then she watched *Sooty*, the haughty, naughty golden bear with a magic wand and the incantation *Izzy wizzy, let's get busy...*

See? Chazza had said, in a meaningful, I-told-you-so voice.

'I don't press her or test her. Sometimes she has the air of an unexploded bomb.'

'I know all about *them*,' said Chazza.

They stood back and watched her, fascinated, thinking of all the oddities that confirmed everything.

Such as the moment with the robin...

Dicky Bird House, Granny had told Lilith when she moved in, had been named after a family of robins, one of which had landed on the fence to come and see the new tenant.

'A long time ago, far from here, a robin plucked a thorn that was hurting him from er...from a *man's* head, yes a special man's head, and a drop of blood fell on the robin's chest and that's why all robins have red breasts now. But believe you me they look sweet, robins do, but they're vicious little creatures and steal the nests of other birds and destroy the eggs. '

Lilith had nodded, as if she knew this stuff.

Granny was glad she didn't have to explain more about the man with the thorn in his head.

The next time the saw the robin it was in the mouth of a local cat which dropped it at Lilith's feet when Granny was showing her around the various vegetable and flower beds in the extensive garden.

Shoo! said Granny to the moggie and did, leaving a bundle of inert feathers with glassy eyes. Granny was about to kick it aside into the long grass but Lilith scooped it up.

'Time is,' she said. 'Time. *Is...*'

The bird seemed to inflate itself like a rubber glove, dropped out of her hands, took some unsteady hops on the ground and flew away. When Granny told Hope about this incident the next day she wondered whether the bird had only been stunned and not really dead.

'Oh come on Granny Gráinne ! Believe. You *know...*'

And she did.

'Are you going to enrol her in Sunday School?'

'Oh god, yes… I will in due course. Then the infant school when she's 5. I'm not sure whether to start using her middle name, Mary, in case some nutter in the village starts asking questions. Or maybe just Lily. But her mum seems to have called her that only when she was smashed. We've all got to keep up appearances and hide in plain sight. In the meantime let her get as much of *Sooty* and *The Clangers* and *The Magic Roundabout* as she can. She loves Dylan the Rabbit. So do I!'

'I clean the vicarage once a month. The vicar fancies me.'

'Do you fancy him?'

'Not a bit.'

Faith looked to the large mirror which had been hung to face the wall, turned it around and pouted into it, touching up her lipstick and then primping her perm.

'Have you dyed your hair? It's not normally that black.'

'Yes with that new L'Oréal *Preference*. I got it from Brown's Hardware shop in town. Only used a couple of gallons. Here, do you think I've put on weight?'

She turned and twisted before the mirror.

'No. Are you pregnant?'

'No but I've gone on that Pill that all the girls are trying. I'll have some fun now...'

'You always did.'

'The vicar told me I was *la belle dame avec hoover* and then explained it to me. To *me*!'

'So he doesn't know you're fluent.'

'We've all got to keep hidden haven't we? Anyway, I plan on letting him seduce me when his wife's not around, then if he ever gives Lilith any grief I'll nail him.'

'Sounds like a plan.'

'He calls our gang The Wise Women of Winturwell and keeps asking why we all don't come to church more often.'

If only he knew... they said in unison, and chuckled.

Faith switched on the telly for the news. The screen was a mass of hissing static.

'It always works for Lilith.'

Lilith was shoving the trowel into the moist earth and loved the hissing sound of metal against wet soil. There were times when she was fully and truly just a little girl bewildered by a missing Mummy; other times, she simply needed to act like one and say the right things. She knew what the two grown-ups were talking about behind the net curtains, and that it was all kind. A side of her (the far side), knew that while they had come to her rescue, she would one day rescue them. Somehow. In a way, her little-girl self was actually protecting *them*.

'And the earth is mine,' she whispered, pushing the tines deeper and levering out a weed and some worms.

She remembered the *Book of Babalon* and a drunken rant from her mother: *Listen Lily, darling darling **darling**, Lily...*

73

that lot out there will tell you: 'The earth is the Lord's, and the fullness thereof.' *from their stupid book. But Verse 57 in* **our** *Book says:* 'And the earth is mine.' *Mine, Lily. And yours one day. Not the useless stupid stupld* **stupid** *Lord's...*

She could still summon up lots of words from Mummy's book but she knew now it wasn't a patch on *Wizards and Witches* by that Enid Lady, with lots of short stories about grumpy wizards and clever elves and a pixie who rode on a rabbit.

One day, she'd write her own stories and the whole world would hear them,

Dig dig dig...

When she had visited the lady Owl earlier she knew that she was hungry but didn't want to hunt when people were around. So Lilith was gathering various insects, three large worms, two small spiders and two slugs that she dropped into an empty tin of Heinz 57 Varieties baked beans, covering the top so they couldn't escape. She wasn't sure whether to tell the prisoners *Time Was* and make them die, but didn't know if Owl preferred live or dead food.

She clambered up to the large nest, her clawed feet holding onto the rough bark of the tree. *This is the last time*, she told the bird. She told it not in words, or in mental pictures, but by a curious sort of auric impulse that lovers use, and spirits with their mediums.

Let grass grow. Mice come. I get. Owl had replied likewise, rather curtly.

Owl gulped down its meal with as much relish as the Clangers had done theirs and then perched, still and upright, offering Lilith its motionless orbs.

In return for the food, Lilith wanted to peer into Owl's huge eyes. Pushing close she matched her own black eyes to the huge dark pupils of the bird; it was like putting her face into the large end of a pair of binoculars. Then she felt a sort of falling inside, her vision flowing down long tubes, travelling to an ancient time when even the Moon was less scarred, converging at small and distant scenes. She could see faraway worlds that even Enid Blyton could never have imagined: Shining people, tall and graceful, wise and angry, kind and murderous; fires and floods and small dark-haired people looking up, and the Big Ones Above looking down. *I know this*, she thought.

An..? Ann..ana..Anu...?

Words, names, trembling on the edge of memory but with a little girl's brain not yet formed enough to bring them through.

Not yet, Owl seemed to tell her, as if aware of where she was trying to spy.

'Do you need any help up there?' called a friendly voice from below. It was Hope, carrying a hamster in a cage, and Chazza behind her carrying a tricycle.

Hope was excited again. She was the youngest of the women, always wearing trendy clothes like her Mummy's horrible friends and always, it seemed to Lilith, to be on the verge of dancing or singing. 'Well, your middle name is *Mary*, you've got a goat named *Mungo* and here is *Midge*... Look, isn't he sweet?' She put the cage on the low wall that bordered the lawn. 'See? There's his little red house in the corner. He drinks water from this feeder here, and he gets in that wheel and goes round and round. You don't need to watch them on the telly now. We've made the real thing happen for you: *Mary, Mungo and Midge.'*

Lilith had stopped watching that programme, having outgrown them already. She looked at the beady-eyed, golden hamster, the wheel and the bars that were so much like the bars of her old cot.

Hello she said, opening the door and letting it jump out, onto the grass. It rolled on its back when it landed and then started to scamper away. With a great WOOSH of wings that made them jump aside, Owl was on it in a flash, grabbed it with feet that were so much like Lilith's and carried it back to its nest.

'Ugh…' said Hope.

Chazza bent double laughing.

'Thank you for the tricycle,' said Lilith, mounting it and riding off along the path toward the edge of the garden where the stream and pond lay.

'Today is market day,' said Granny one morning. 'This is how I make a living.'

Lilith frowned. She didn't understand either of those concepts. She had never seen any grown-up actually going out to earn money and had never handled the stuff. In some ways she wasn't much further advanced in life than Midge the short-lived hamster had been.

In fact Granny was not being totally honest. While she did indeed take her stuff to the markets in the Five Towns, she never earned enough to make a living. Lilith's 'best mummy in the world', in one of her cogent moments, felt that regular payments into Gráinne 's bank account would do more for the little girl than anything she could have done. And she was right about that

So after feeding Mungo, which she did every morning whether Goat was hungry or not, Lilith helped Granny take her produce up to the old Land Rover. At the top of the path she paused and looked back at the valley that was half-filled with a deep river of dirty-silver mist. A part of her wanted to just dive into it and see if unusual creatures lived there, as they do in the night, but she heard Granny's call to put her new boots on that Faith had brought.

'Remember,' Granny said as she laced them up for her, 'other people must not see your feet. They are special feet, magic feet, as you are a special girl. But other people, ordinary people, no matter how nice they are, might not understand. Do *you* understand?'

Lilith nodded. Granny's face, level with hers, was shining.

'Now what comes next, eh?'

'Clunk, click, every trip...'

76

The Thursday Market was held in a car park next to the river. Granny didn't have a stall to assemble like others traders, who sold cheeses and fishes and meats and sweets. Instead she unfolded what she called paste tables, covered them with shiny green fake grass cloths and spread out her own produce, marked with a hand painted sign that said 'Home Grown'. Chazza had told her that 'Organic' was the coming term, but that seemed a bit too pretentious and she felt it would never catch on. She had apples, beans, carrots, blackberries, strawberries, some raspberries, Brussels sprouts and potatoes. And best of all she had a lockable box for money. Lilith was fascinated by the shiny half-crowns, sixpences, shillings, huge brown pennies and thrupenny bits. There was talk of these being made obsolete by new decimal currency, but if the Governor of the Bank of England had seen the delight with which a certain little girl was handling these, he'd have binned the changeover.

'Twelve of these big brown pennies are the same as this silver shilling. And twenty of these shillings are the same as this paper one called a pound note. So there are – a big number coming up - two hundred and forty pennies in a pound.'

Lilith nodded. She always nodded. Granny hadn't yet decided whether she learnt with prodigious speed, or was just agreeing as the easy option.

The market was busy. The sun had brought people out. A lot of them looked at Lilith and smiled. A few commented: 'What a pretty little girl!' and Granny glowed. With her smart boots, blue dungarees that had turn-ups, bright red top and long, silky black hair tumbling down over her pure white face from her own brimmed hat, Lilith looked as if she had stepped from a fairy tale.

Since Granny had brought her to the valley she had known what it was to feel safe and wanted. But there was now a *new* feeling floating around in her chest, here in the marketplace, that was probably the best of all. Because of the stories Granny and the Three Wise Women read and told, and the nursery rhymes and silly songs, and all the nice, exciting adventures she had seen on the telly, this one had to be what they called... er, Happiness? Is this how this world works, she thought? Is this what I have to feel?

She found herself making strange croaking noises like the frogs in the pond near the bee-hives.

Granny came dashing across, thinking she was choking on something, ready to turn her upside-down or do the Heimlich manoeuvrer or even phone 999 from the nearby telephone box. Then she realised what it was:

'Goodness Lilith...you're laughing. I've never heard you laugh before.'

Lilith nodded her usual nod.

'*You're* crying.'

'Nonsense! Stuff. And. Nonsense. Now go and say hello to the swans while I sort out my King Edwards for this nice man. Don't go through the railings and don't go wandering off!'

'Clunk Click, Granny.'

Behind the set-up of their tables was a narrow path, a verge, railings, and beyond that the greeny-black river that was almost clogged with reeds in places. She rested her chin on the cold metal of the railing and watched a green double-decker bus chugging over the old town bridge. For a moment she thought she saw the boy again, at the front, peering down at her for the two seconds it took to turn off out of sight. But then she saw the two large swans and three smaller swans flowing up to where she stood and that was far more interesting.

'Hello,' she said, and something flowed back that echoed the greeting.

When she had looked through the eyes of Owl, down and back into a primal world where the stars and Moon were different, and even the people were not quite as they were here in the market place, these scenes acted upon the far side of her like the children's programme. They reminded of things that she probably shouldn't have forgotten, or helped teach her how this new world worked.

The far side of Lilith knew that she had once known so very much, but it was all so very far away. Even so, without being able to put it into words she knew that Owl – all Owls – was there to serve her. She just knew that. And she felt – no she *knew* – that if she wanted to order the birds and beasts and even the flowers around her, like the Matron had done with the lost and lonely children, then she could.

She would never become like Matron though. Sister Ndlovu had taught her to be kind. And she would always be kind to the things in her life that *weren't* human, even the scary things that floated around the astral night-time realms. She hadn't been upset about the hamster. It hated being in its cage, was actually quite ill, and seemed to say *Time Was* to her through its beady black eyes. Then Owl did the rest.

Lilith was about to ask the Swans if they could tell her anything about herself, when she felt someone next to her putting one foot on hers, as if by accident. She tried to move but her foot was trapped. She knew that this man with a shirt and tie, blue blazer, creased trousers and a sharp parting in his short hair, was actually trying to feel the shape of her toes.

'Hello, little girl,' he said, in a lovely soft voice, too soft for anyone else in the market to hear. 'Nice swans, yeah? They stay together for life, did you know that? I can tell you all sorts of things about them. Can I buy you some sweeties?' He looked behind to see that granny was still busy with a customer, then took her hand and dragged her in the opposite direction to the sweet stall.

She might have cried out. She might have tried to find the far side of herself but she didn't have to. All Lilith saw was a massive flurry of pure whiteness that freed his grip. The whole market, the whole town as far as the war memorial heard the hissing, honking sound the pen swan made as she flew up and attacked the man.

Everyone in the market turned to look.

'You bad girl!' shouted the man. 'You threw stones at those poor swans! You need - '

He didn't finish, just walked briskly across the road and around the corner without looking back. Lilith ran to Granny's outstretched arms.

'Bad girl,' muttered some in the crowd who only saw and judged by the finish of things and never the start.

The old man with the bag of King Edward potatoes hefted them into his sholley and warned Granny:

'She might look sweet, but she'll grow up into a real monster if you're not careful.'

'Oh I do hope so!' she replied through gritted teeth.

The work of the image, and the potion and the charm, the work of the spider and the snake, and the little ones that go in the dark, this is your work

The Book of Babalon

In the garden, there were small places where Time stood still. Or if not stand still, exactly, so much as not exist at all. Granny's parents noticed this when they came for sanctuary during the War and felt obliged to warn their daughter.

'Gráinne , there's something about this place that isn't quite kosher.'

Which meant, of course, that she fell in love with the acreage and its random slopes immediately.

'Stuff and nonsense, Dad,' she retorted. 'You can go back to the doodlebugs if you want.'

In fact she knew exactly where these places were. One was in an area just beyond the canes for the French beans; another was further toward the manor, on a small mound she called The Hump, perched like a boil on a sharp slope that would never yield more than dandelions.

Years later, a boyfriend encouraged her to try this thing he called meditation, and extolled its virtues of stillness, mindlessness, peacefulness; of being centred and totally aware. She knew that she could get all of this just by sitting in these spots in the garden.

The boyfriend was a younger man who dressed like a Hippy, wore a Zapata moustache and liked to be known as Zak, although his name was really Nigel. Being what he termed a New Ager, Zak sensed that there were spiritual potentials within Gráinne and hoped that he might help her catch up and perhaps join the Liberal party with him.

We could become like the immortal lovers Diarmuid and Gráinne in Irish mythology.

No Zak, I don't think they ended well.

Didn't they? Well maybe me and you should, you know…

No.

In fact what he sniffed from Gráinne was the spiritual equivalent of her car's burning oil when she was already beyond him and a long way ahead. Over the years he had tried to woo her with horoscopes, gems, crystals, tarot cards, corn dollies, and offers of what he called Weed. She was interested in none of these: the only weeds that concerned her were those that threatened her crops. But he had been kind, and no trouble, and she had sometimes felt a teensy bit guilty for the various moments she had – slightly – used him.

Even so, he was nothing if not persistent. He had written to her recently (in the days when people did still write), and put a first class stamp on the envelope, recommending a book about a shaman called Don Juan Matus, who leaped into the darkness from a height and entered into another realm.

Stuff and nonsense, she had written back using a second-class stamp, although she felt sure that if she ever leapt from that Hump toward the Moon, into the darkness of the valley, then she'd travel very far indeed.

'You haven't found your Path, Gráinne. You can be so uncool. Wake up! Lighten up!' he had written.

If only he knew… Gráinne 's path was as old as the world and the people on it. There were times when she had followed it through darkest forest and over the razor-sharp mountain ridges of sunken lands, while all the time doing a real job in the outer world, without thought of reward other than one day bringing something to pass via Lilith.

Of course, when Lilith was first turned loose in the garden she made a bee-line for these two places and just stood there, swaying gently in some akashic breeze. Gráinne left her alone. It would never do to tell her Who she was, or Where she really came from. 90% of her was still just a tiny little girl without enough of the ordinary things she needed to learn in order to survive.

'She seems to be a tiny bit straighter,' observed Hope, who had come down after finishing a shift at the old Chest Hospital on top of their hill and was still in her uniform. 'Her little legs...they're straightening by the day.'

'I think she's decided that this is how she wants to be. You know how my arthritic fingers were beginning to twist? I mentioned them to Lilith and overnight, during sleep, something was done and *now* look at them, straight as arrows! Maybe I'm imagining it though.' She spread her fingers and looked at the light through them, closed and opened again then clenched them into a fist. 'Maybe it's Lilith helping me to fix myself.'

'Believe, Granny Gráinne, believe!'

'Oh I do. Plus she gets lots of exercise and fresh air now, so maybe that helps too.'

'I've got her a couple of lovely little dresses and a gorgeous coat for when it gets cold.'

'Don't spoil her.'

'Try and stop me! Does she still quote that ridiculous *Book of Babalon*?'

'Not so much. But there are times when I think she has to stop herself.'

'I read through that copy you showed us and there isn't much in the way of happiness is there? A bit of joy and a lot of ecstasy. What do *you* think of it? Is it really stuff and nonsense, as you tell her?'

'I'd give it three out of ten – maybe four. I'd tell the writer to go away, trim it down and then work at it even more. When he channelled it, I think that Parsons was in the grip of a tortured and tormenting relationship. I think he hoped to impress his woman and sway her back toward him.'

'Ooh I'd like a fella like that!'

'I must introduce you to Zak.'

'Is he handsome?'

'No.'

'Don't bother.'

'I might try and edit the book myself one day, if you'd all help me. After all, it is sort of *her* book, and predicted her coming. We can keep the good bits and create our own for the four lines that are missing.'

'That would be fun. We could rename it the *Book of Lilith.* Can we keep the joy and ecstasy in?'

'Bring some gin and tonic and we'll have a blast.'

If Lilith had been a young woman entering university she would spend three years learning from a rigid curriculum of courses leading from A to Z. They would be delivered by professors at set times in coherent blocks of learning and she would have to master all the terms and technicalities in approved ways. Here in the valley that was her university she had 'nine moons' before she needed to start infant school: a stretch of existence that to a little girl was a sizeable portion of infinity.

She learned a lot from Owl and sometimes she could see pictures of what she thought of as the First Times. But they were like the thousand-piece jigsaws that Granny liked to do. At the moment, perching as she was on the tree, the pieces were heaped and scattered at random and she still hadn't found the corners and straight bits that would help it make sense.

Another teacher was Snake. In fact she probably liked him more than Owl though she did have to tell the latter not to swoop down and eat him. His skin had a black and yellow collar behind his head like a slipped crown. He showed her how he shed his whole skin, and his glazed turquoise eyes as he did so reminded her of a people who were very different to those around her now. When she looked into them it was like looking through a narrow crack that wouldn't stay open longer than a blink.

Goat didn't teach much with those strange pupils that saw everywhere but was happy to be ridden and seemed to keep watch on her. She was quite sure that if anyone sneaked into the garden to be cruel then Mungo Goat would leap up and drive them away. One day she would write a story about a little girl who rode Goat into the starlight of other worlds. Or perhaps she had already done that? she sometimes wondered.

And then there were the trees, who seemed to whisper stories up from the roots and shiver them down through their leaves: stories about the people who had lived here in the valley, where not all of them were kind or good, and many of them struggled. Granny had given her a toy watering can and sometimes she went around each of the trees in the garden watering the roots, telling those people *My star is in thee* as her Mummy used to say, and although she didn't exactly know what that meant she hoped it would bring them peace. Once, Chazza had come down the path and seen her doing that and said, nicely: *But shouldn't you be doing the vegetables Lilith?* Chazza didn't understand.

At the far western end of the garden, there was a the small broken gate in the low dry stone wall, at either side of which were the two apple trees that she must never pass. When Granny had told her that, Lilith had seen her pull a face and think silently: *Of course she will go past them! What a stupid thing to say!* As damage limitation she added:

'Listen Lilith, it's not that there's anything special there, it's just that the grounds of the manor begin at that gate. It is private property and while Sir Hugh and Lady E. are very nice people, they don't want to be interrupted. Our land used to be theirs but it became too much for them when they got older and so our family bought it. Please stay put. Be kind to neighbours.'

Yes granny, clunk click, she had lied, having every intention of going there at the right moment.

If it is a cliché that every adult has a small child within; it is a cliché because it is true. But every adult also has a whole sequence of old gates into the past that probably shouldn't be opened unless you know exactly where they will lead. The very act of opening them enables us to step through into very different realms. Some of these can be frowning, sinister places that yet hide treasure. Others can seem shiny and golden but paved with cobblestones of hurt and loss.

It was warm when Lilith sneaked out in the darkness toward that broken gate in the low dry-stone wall, next to the two apple trees that Granny said she must avoid. She was still in her white nightie with her budgie mirror dangling from her neck, but barefoot. It was fun being a little girl but there were moments when the Big Person would not be denied and opened its own gate to come through.

She remembered a line from Mummy's book: *This is the way of it, star, star. Burning bright, moon, witch moon.* This was night, this was her realm.

Be still she said to the wind and it stilled. Starlight fell upon her like rain and if the actual Moon wasn't yet risen in the sky its secret far side was blazing full and red.

The gate, broken-hinged, wouldn't swing open. She climbed over it. She was good at climbing and had caused Granny many fearful moments when she had scaled trees to talk to Owl or check on the robins and squirrels to see if they needed anything. *Be kind to neighbours*, Granny had said, and as far as she was concerned this meant all life, not just the human.

Beyond the gate, still clustered by trees and shrubs, a small rivulet ran down the hillside to eventually tumble into the distant canal. This was what she had heard in the night, with her excellent hearing: a constant tinkling like the faery bells in the stories she had absorbed.

Other than from a tap, she had never seen free running water before. She put her hand in and marvelled at its silver. She washed her face and felt very old, somehow, as if touching upon all the people before who had done exactly this, at this spot. The frail side of her brought up the bad memories of her time in London; now she washed and shuddered them away and was no longer angry. Then she dipped one foot into a little pool the waters made before tumbling onward. She tried to see her reflection once the ripples had stilled and was being very calm, very careful because she knew she was being watched from the other side of the streamlet.

She saw him out of the corner of her eye. The little boy. Dressed in white but hidden behind a shrub, so she couldn't make out details. When she looked full on he disappeared. Then when she turned away and did that thing with the side of her eyes that Goat could do, she could see his face carved in moonlight, clear as daylight: long white hair, one blue eye and one green. Small mouth. A sad, worried expression.

Poor thing, she thought, and tried to glimpse him through her mirror, angling it all ways and peering from different angles.

Don't hide she said.

He hid more. Only the eyes were now visible from between the branches of the shrub.

I'm Lilith. Who are you?

A rustling of leaves and he was gone.

She wasn't going to follow. It wouldn't have felt right. Besides a light had come on in the upper room of Dicky Bird House, which meant that Granny had woken up and would come looking for her with a big torch, terrified, telling her off, carrying her back to bed and sitting on the end of it until she had to pretend to sleep so that Granny herself could drop off.

'She's a strange little thing,' said Granny to Chazza the next morning while Lilith zoomed back and forth along the paths on her tricycle.

'We'd be disappointed if she wasn't.'

'She sneaked out last night and headed toward the apple trees. I asked her where she had been and what she had been doing but all I got was Nowhere and Nothing.'

'Typical child,' they said in unison.

Chazza turned the mirror around and tried to find something in her features she could still admire. She was incapable of leaving the house in the morning, even just to put the bin out, without applying her make-up. Lately, she felt she needed more and more.

'I'm getting old,' she said.

'I'd be surprised if you didn't.'

'I'm hoping to find a good fella before it's too late.'

'You've been saying that for years. I should fix you up with Zak.'

'Is he well hung?'

'No.'

'Don't bother. But you know, Gráinne, you don't seem to have as many wrinkles now.'

'Ridiculous,' she laughed, but pushed her aside to see for herself, then secretly looked at her straightened fingers before turning the mirror back to the wall.

'Still worried about that superstition?'

'Which one? About all mirrors leading to Lilith's cave? I'm not taking any chances. You know how these things go...'

Gráinne certainly knew how such things went, and that myths have their own reality. Myths can be like golems. We create them out of imagined needs, to feed ourselves on long journeys, imbuing lifeless clay with that intangible spark sometimes called a soul. And then they go lurching on down the centuries through war and peace, stability and chaos, terror and bliss.

She knew that a golem had been created within Jewish lore that spoke of Lilith as being Adam's first wife, created from the same clay. They had lived happily in Eden until Adam tried to show that he was the boss. Lilith refused to lay beneath him during sex, proclaiming that as they were both equal, both from the dust of the earth, she should not be expected to do this. Then she left to live her own life. When

89

Adam whined to God about her departure, he sent three angels to retrieve her. They found Lilith in a cave bearing children but Lilith refused to come back to the garden. The angels told her they would kill 100 of her children every day for her disobedience. Since then, in revenge, she became the bat-winged Night Monster who was held responsible for the deaths of still-born infants and otherwise inexplicable cot-deaths. She became the sexually wanton Night Demon who seduced the holy men in their unholy dreams.

Stuff and nonsense and taradiddle! Granny Gráinne had often thundered, railing at this version of what we now call False News. *Her* Lilith, the *real* Lilith, was not mud-born but star-born. She came from a realm that was far older and stranger than anything understood by the circumcising wretches who wrote the Talmud or Torah, or those tedious little men at Qumran who fancied that they were Sons of Light and blamed her for their nocturnal emissions.

If she turned the mirrors around in their little house it was not because of myths involving a Jewish Lilith in her cave, but because she didn't want the little girl's real origins to come spurting out yet.

It was the unexploded bomb thing, all over again.

It was inevitable, as part of Lilith's very own and very 'open' university education, that she stumbled upon the bats. Of course they found her, every dusk, when they emerged from what used to be quarried caves to go hunting: midges, small moths, flies, beetles, small wasps and spiders. Right from her arrival in the valley she saw them flitting around the house at dusk but was too busy with other aspects of her earthchildly curriculum to get close.

The butterfly net was still implanted at the side of the path and fluttered emptily in any breeze showing strength and direction. Granny used it to decide whether it was worthwhile hanging out the washing that day or leaving it on a folding rack next to the fire. 'I wonder...' she muttered when she glanced outside and saw the long fine-meshed tube twitching in a way that wasn't caused by any butterfly, no matter how large. Then excitedly: 'Come with me, Lilith... But put some slippers on in case the postie sees you. He's due any moment.'

They hurried outside and up the path. Lilith climbed on top of the low wall to be level with the mouth of the net and Granny rolled up her sleeves, opening it carefully, then reached in and down, fumbling with something and withdrawing it. She held the creature in her two big hands cupped like a cave. Then she opened a tiny gap between her thumbs so that Lilith could peek inside.

Lilith said nothing. Just stood there with open mouth, breathing deeply. With its grey-brown fur, mouse-like face with an odd noseleaf and pointed ears, it was the most beautiful thing she had ever seen.

'This is a lesser horse-shoe bat. It lives in caves near here that used to be quarries, where they cut out Bath Stone. You should be pleased because these bats are protected by law. This whole area is called a Site of Special Scientific Interest because of them.'

Lilith was pleased. She still couldn't speak. Instead she told the tiny plum-sized creature with folded wings: *Don't be scared.*

'It's not scared, is it?' mused Granny as she carefully, very gently, opened one wing and then the other to show Lilith. 'It reminds me of how you looked when I first came to get you.'

'Thank you.'

'See its wings? Its tiny legs? It can't take off from the ground like birds, so it hangs upside down and takes flight that way. It really does sleep in the day and wake at night to go hunting. Then it goes back to its cave to hang upside down. Safe from just about everything that might want to eat it.'

'I can hear it squeaking. It's tired. It wants to go home.'

'My goodness you've got good ears!'

Granny opened her hands and offered the bat up to the sky and it flew off, zig-zagging beyond the trees.

'I will take you to its cave next week but you must – MUST – promise never to go by yourself. There are bad people around, and even good people might cause trouble if they thought I let a little girl like you wander all over the place by herself. Promise.'

She did, and she meant it this time. She would never want to get Granny into trouble.

'But I want wings like that some day.'

'I think you've probably already got some, somewhere.'

Lilith found her wings that same night. Instead of standing at her bedroom window and peering out in vision at the otherworldly denizens cavorting like fish in a tank, she suddenly knew what to do. She opened the window and lay down on her bed and waited patiently, knowing that Bat would come in, and Bat did. It – she - fluttered around the room and hooked it's feet, so much like Lilith's own feet, onto the lilac tassels of the lampshade.

Hello, she said. *Thank you.*

Bat stretched its wings and with Lilith's excellent eyesight in the dark, she marvelled at the translucent membrane of skin which connected the forearm and elbow and long long fingers with its thumb on the wing's top edge.

I want wings

You can have them.

Yes, Yes I can.

We all can, as Lilith would show us. These days there are generations of folk who travel the realms by assuming god-forms, or developing and projecting their *ka* or stepping from the flesh in simple astral bodies of light, or visualising themselves in animal forms which can be sent scurrying over the night lands to spy. Or more often they create these new-fangled merkabas around themselves which spin and flow and take you where you need to be in all the worlds, all at once. Or if, like Lilith, they simply want to add wings just for effect then these appear.

Lilith found stepping out of her body easy, and she felt the simple, gentle, light ecstasy we all know when it happens . She looked down at herself on the bed, legs straight, arms folded on her chest, the teddy hot water bottle next to her head. And then around the whole room that was luminous with colours that most people will only ever see in story books or on a cinema screen.

Hello said Bat, but it had Granny's voice. *You didn't know I could do this, did you?*

The Big Person within her did, and had always known, though sometimes she had needed to forget it while learning to be an *Earth*girl.

One of us is always around at night, looking after you. In one form or another. Some would call us your Guardian Angels but we're more than that.

Thank you.

Now where do you want to go? Just think of the place and you will be there. Every place is within you.

I want to go to the Moon.

And so they did...

My vessel must be perfect. This is the way of her perfection

The Book of Babalon

It was the vicar's wife, Miriam Figge, who ran the Sunday School. Gráinne and the three guardians had debated at some length whether Lilith really needed to attend. In the event they agreed, reluctantly, that it would be a gentle inoculation that might prepare her for the hurly-burly of the Infants School.

Lilith was cuddled on Aunty Hope's lap on the couch, watching the telly. She pretended to be engrossed in *Catweazle*, which was about a wizard from the 11th century who accidentally finds himself in the year 1969 with his familiar, a toad called Touchwood. Really, she was listening to every word they said, although a teeny tiny part of her did think she'd like a pet toad.

The Big People in the room were not worried that Lilith might be converted or corrupted by the Christian orthodoxy, but that she might get found out. One day, when she was prepared, she would have to reveal everything to all; now was not the time.

As for Lilith herself, well, she might commune with almost every bird, beast, vegetable, tree and flower within the garden, not to mention an unusual array of inner plane beings that Gráinne and co. kept their own third-eyes on, but there was a side of her that quite liked the idea of finding a friend of her own age with whom she could race tricycles, or run along the fields and lanes shouting and waving and making dens.

Hope must have felt her thoughts: a tiny exhalation of loneliness. So while giving Lilith an extra hug she then suggested:

'Maybe there's a side of her that wants to find a friend of her own age so she can race tricycles, or run along the fields and lanes, shouting like mad things and making dens.'

Chazza snorted: 'You mean find a little friend of her own age who is, what, 5,000 years old?'

Four pairs of eyes met and formed an equi-armed cross within the room. They agreed. It had to start sometime.

'It's been fun!' they said in unison.

They held the Sunday School in a porta-kabin in the centre of the old part of the village. Lilith was taken there the first time by Chazza who would be quite happy to head-butt Mrs Miriam Figge at the slightest sign of any nonsense. And then she was given whispered final instructions that were every bit as terse as some of those in the *Book of Babalon:*

*Don't **ever** mention the name Babalon.*

*Your name is **Lily**, not Lilith.*

*No matter what happens, if anything goes wrong, **DON'T use your power** to fix things.*

And most of all – what is most of all? - Tell me?

Never never never take my shoes off. Never never.

Chazza patted her head then bent down to give her a kiss.

'Oh you're such a clever little girl.,

'Thank you,' she said, and ran her fingers over the crow's feet of her aunty's eyes.

'Oh Lily...If only they knew...'

Earlier on that day Faith did *her* bit by going to the church and listened intently to the Reverend Michael Figge's sermon. She sat on an empty row, half-way down the aisle, and there was no-one in front. She stood, uncertainly, when she was told; and sat, hesitantly, when the others did. She was so obviously unfamiliar with church services that she was crying out to be saved. But she did sing heartily with a fine contralto that rather overpowered the thin limping notes from the very sparse congregation

More than that, she never once took her eyes off the vicar and didn't seem to care who noticed. He felt himself blushing. Everyone saw.

Who does she think she is? came a few whispers from the old ladies with large hats, clustered in the pews further back.

Actually, **who** *is she?*

The Reverend Michael Figge knew her as the woman they employed to clean the vicarage, who liked to be called Faith. This, as far as he knew, was her first time in church. It struck him that she was heavily made-up. Her lipstick, on her cupid lips, looked like a burning bow. He tried hard not to stare. Everyone noticed. Miriam never used make-up. *Au naturel* he used to joke, and tried hard to admire, but sometimes he wished his wife could be a little less austere.

He spent all his time thinking about Faith.

In truth, in very truth, or *verily*, as Jesus used to say when He wanted to insist on things, he spent more time thinking about Faith than he did about God.

Typical of that era, he and his wife were a childless middle class couple who lived in an upper class vicarage on a lower class income. He also ran the small local primary school, so he had a lot on his hands. Even so, when Faith suggested the house was too large to clean in just one visit per month he persuaded Miriam that fortnightly was needed – at very least. Miriam, who assumed Faith was too stupid to know that her hourly rate was ridiculously low, even said: *Why not come weekly?* Which meant that she could join the great and the good of the valley and have moveable feasts of canasta or Mahjong at their houses.

Thank you God, the Reverend Figge had whispered, hoping that even God wouldn't hear that.

He spent all his time thinking about Faith. She was a good woman who, despite her low earnings, had even paid for special orthopaedic shoes for the odd little niece that he would one day welcome into his school.

In slow ways, to his astonishment, she seemed to align herself more closely to him. She pressed against him, one bosom against his shoulder-blade when he was poring over his next sermon. He had a high opinion of women and believed that they had superior insight, although he had (reluctantly) excepted Miriam from this. Even though he was mouldering into his barren 50s, with thinning hair and increasing gut, he believed that Faith, especially, could see through to the real man: strong, brilliant, sensual and pure. Inwardly he was a Muscular Christian, more Marlon Brando than Mr Pastry. He daydreamed about reading his hidden copy of *Lady Chatterley's Lover* to her, and watching her glow, and come toward him, smiling.

Silly, silly man he told himself often, yet he lived for the days when she turned up with her hoover and mops and set to work. Several times he sat at his desk and each time he felt the bosom again as she leaned over, intrigued by his depth of insight, asking him about the hard words. He had declared her as *La Belle Dame avec Hoover* and she had blushed, and he intuited that she probably hadn't had much kindness from *real* men.

'I never see you in church, Faith.'

She gave him the saddest look, slipped on the Marigolds and went back to her cleaning. So when she appeared this time, made up to the nines (as they used to say), it was like an open declaration of love.

For years The Reverend Figge had been an essentially sad man who observed life with his face pushed up against the glass. He could see what was going on among the modern folk but couldn't join in. He saw it all happening but he wasn't there. He wanted to be everyone's friend but was rarely more than just a vicar, an acquaintance, a necessary habit for his increasingly diminishing congregation.

Even his church's saint, Saint Barbara, had been one of the 93 recently demoted by the cads in Rome. From being venerated for centuries as a noble martyr from Baalbek (from where all manner of ancient demons sprang), her very existence was now being denied.

So where, spiritually, did that leave him?

He thought of Faith.

All the time.

Lilith quite liked being Lily. Or, looking at it in a differing light from the far side of the Moon, then Lily was quite happy not to be Lilith. She understood how important both sides were.

Their little Sunday School was quite well attended by over a dozen children, ranging in ages from 3 to 12. These children were nice to Lily and were not like the damaged monsters in the Home. The class listened to the simple stories, did drawings and paintings and made collages and never thought to challenge their very attendance, or what they were being taught. This was 30 years or more before the accessibility of the Google Monster, and its facility for taking large axes to the roots of blind faith:

*Does God **really** exist?*

*How was the world **really** made?*

*Did Adam and Eve **really** exist?*

*Was there **really** a big Flood?*

Lilith actually knew the answers to all of these; but Lily was happy to keep quiet and listen to the stories and join in with the drawing and painting and milk and biscuits afterwards. She became quite good at the drawing and painting, though often wouldn't stick to the topic.

Mrs Figge asked:

Why do you keep drawing big snake eyes in the sky, Lily?

Lily always shrugged.

Why have you drawn Noah's Ark like a big, er, er...spaceship?

More shrugs.

Why is it in the sky and not on the waters?

No answer, just another splash of poster paint on the paper to show huge dark waves. She wondered if the child might have this condition she'd just heard of known as 'autism' and decided to find out more.

But these were all tiny challenges made by Mrs Figge. To the world at large, the vicar's dour wife did no more than dutifully reflect her husband's light; yet she sometimes caught swirls of luminance from her own far side. In the presence of Lily, they became quite bright, although she couldn't exactly tell where they emanated from.

Although Lily was obviously *unusual* in appearance and manner, she was no trouble. The fact that she said very little while seeming to understand all, made her enormously intriguing. Once, she had told the class about the importance of saying Please, Thank You and Sorry. When she asked if anyone had any questions it was dark-eyed Lily who had asked:

Does God say Please?

Does God say Thank You?

Does God say Sorry?

Miriam Figge suddenly felt as if she was standing like The Fool on a high cliff. She didn't know the answer to that. So she did what she had done many times: she smiled, said that when she was a big girl she'd understand; then offered everyone more biscuits.

And very often, after engaging with Lily as much as the girl allowed, she came away feeling… clean. As if she'd had some kind of psychic shower.

Every week she looked forward to the Sunday School.

And she started to think of Lily.

All the time.

Gráinne and the Guardians had no antagonism toward the Church in any of its forms. Nor were they the sort who adorned their homes with pentagrams or Green Men or *Sheila na Gigs* and corn dollies while keeping up with the solstices and equinoxes and Quarter Days. There had been, in fact, rumours of witchcraft within the valley, centred around bonfires in the woods near the caves, but this was nothing to do with *Our* Ladies, if we may call them that. As women of the intra-class, they looked upon the Figges of this world as being like the men with red flags who used to walk in front of motor cars.

They were in Dicky Bird House, looking out through the net curtains at Lilith talking to Badger, who had just come lumbering through. All agreed that it was going well at Sunday School and that the Reverend Michael Figge would be controlled by Faith by the time Lily Lilith entered Junior School. As for Mrs Figge, Chazza confirmed that the woman was being completely enraptured by her latest pupil.

'Nothing we can do about that,' said Granny. 'Lilith just has to sit still, say nothing, do nothing and she's still a magnet.'

'There was a scary moment when I picked her up yesterday. The idiot vicar decided to come in carrying helium balloons to give out. Full of himself. Probably had a bit of your tit, Faith. Each balloon with the name of St. Barbara on and carrying a label bearing the church's address.'

'Oh shit…'

'Exactly. "A balloon race!" he says. "Everyone put their names on the label and we'll release them. The one that goes the furthest gets a prize!"'

'Sounds like fun,' said Hope.

'It did until the pillock started a chant of *Bar Bar Barbara.*'

'And it reminded Lily of *Ba Ba Babalon* that her mum used to chant.'

'Honest, Gráinne, you could see her start to change. I don't know who or what caused it, but suddenly all the balloons popped with these huge bangs. I used that as an excuse to grab

Lily and get her outside and hold her and stop her doing – you know what.'

'The vicar was mortified. There he was hoping to impress and suddenly he was surrounded by screaming kids and irate mums. He cried: "Don't know what happened there, peoples! Sorreeee! The room must have been too hot. That's Miriam's fault. Anyway, Saint Barbara is the patron saint of artillerymen, so I think she was having a laugh and showing her approval!"'

'That's actually a clever get-out,' said Hope.

'Flaming idiot,' said Chazza.

'Oh he's not bad, really. He really isn't,' came Faith. 'Anyway Granny, what's next on our agenda?'

'We'll find that fella who tried to grab Lilith at the market.'

'What then?'

'Then we'll kill him.'

This for a time appointed. Seek not the end, I
shall instruct thee in my way. But be true. Would
it be hard if I were thy lover, and before thee?
But I am thy lover and I am with thee.

The Book of Babalon

Like sailors and their tides, with all the swirling currents,
anyone who has ever worked the land will know its rhythms.
Granny could walk out into the garden every morning and say
to it: *Come on, what have you to tell me today?* Without fail it
would respond, in a million differing ways. And although it
might be another cliché, this was done with her gut and not
her head. Every Spring, for example, she would break the soil
with her flat hoe and a surge of greeting would flow up the
wooden handle from the very depths of the earth.

Zak could see this in her and tried to talk about her root,
sacral and the ajna chakras, but all she said was her invariable:
'Stuff. And. Nonsense!'. She was fond of Zak in her own way
but knew that his primary aim was to get inside her big white
knickers. And in that time, on the edge of the 1970s, there
were any number of New Age wanna-bes using spirituality as
a means of seduction. As the old joke went, at her age she
could do without sex but she really couldn't do without her
glasses.

'You know, Gráinne,' he almost snapped once, 'If you'd
been around at the time of the Entry into Jerusalem, when all
the other women were crying *Hosanna!* at the sight of Jesus,
you'd have just shouted Stuff and Nonsense!'

'That's truer than you realise, Zak. Now will you help me with the sprouts?'

This particular day, after what became known in the village as 'Vicar Figge's 21-gun Salute' via all the popping balloons, she had two things she needed to ponder:

How best to deal with the Market Man who had tried to snatch Lilith;

What to make of this 'Saint Barbara', about whom she had never given one second of thought until now.

Of the two, it was the latter who exercised most attention. Gráinne was pretty moot as regards reincarnation. But she did believe that the universe consisted of various scripts, and that we can be continuations of certain energies and entities. Was this Saint Barbara from the 3rd Century just such a continuation, echoing down today? She'd have to think on that, and see what it might reveal – if anything. The universe – her universe at least – was also capable of being a Joker.

'Help me get some apples Lilith,' she said that morning, and with the girl's special wellies on they strolled hand in hand toward the end of the garden with two large plastic buckets. For all Granny's otherworldly mien, she loved just putting her hand out to one side and feeling her granddaughter's tiny hand docking into it, like space-capsules were beginning to do above them. When she started to think of the times when her own daughter Victoria used to do the same, she had to stop the memories dead. For all Granny's praeterhuman talents, she felt human disappointments and thoughts of things gone wrong just as acutely as anyone.

As they walked along the narrow path she could feel Lilith's engagement with the seen and the unseen. She was also aware of the strong pull toward the Forbidden Zone where the apple trees grew. Lilith would go there today, but not alone. Besides:

'We're going to make some cider. Down here they call it Scrumpy. We'll bottle it and sell it at the market. It'll make lots of money and we'll get you some new clothes.'

There was definitely a change of tone in the atmosphere just beyond the little gate: like you get at the seaside when the low tide is about to turn. It was never malign, but just had almost sad undertones of *leave me alone.* For herself, Granny was quite happy with anything eldritch, but Lilith's glimpse of the Little Boy when she first arrived made her wary. She didn't know who – or what – that boy was. Or where he might tempt her.

When Lilith gathered the windfall apples she put them into the bucket neatly, almost stacking them as if they had been bricks.

'Just dump them in, Lilith. We're gonna chop them up anyway.'

'No,' said Lilith quietly, and carried on placing, almost as though she had a quiet explanatory word with each one.

'You're a strange little thing,' said Granny.

'Thank you,' said Lilith, knowing that this was meant as the highest praise.

At no time did Lilith peer around for the boy. Either the boy was not there and she knew it, or she was no longer interested.

Granny felt it wiser not to ask.

Chazza turned up with a book she had stolen from the local Reference Library about the lives of saints.

'Go feed Goat, give him a ride and maybe talk to Owl and Snake, Lilith. We'll start making Scrumpy later.'

They watched as she went toward the Hump and sort of danced around it as though she had lots of unseen friends there, looking into her budgie mirror at various angles.

'Strange little thing,' said Chazza, approvingly. 'Anyway, I know you'd be interested in this, Granny,' she muttered, handing the thick book across after wiping it with her hanky. 'I had to wedge it under my armpit and fasten my thick coat up to the neck. You'd be amazed how much a girl can conceal in her armpit when it comes to shop-lifting.'

As Gráinne turned the pages to the first entry under B, Chazza turned the main mirror around to look at herself. 'Hmm...definitely a few less lines today. If we could bottle Lilith we'd make a fortune. Maybe in future I'll invent something we can inject to get rid of wrinkles. Wotcher think? No, I mean about Saint Barbara...'

Granny Gráinne was intrigued. Saints and their deeds had as much substance for her as gurus and their Masters: little different to those balloons which had popped.

'Now this is odd. Barbara actually means 'foreign'. If she did exist, then she is described as being from Baalbek – which is where *You Know Who* came from.'

'*Big* Lilith, you mean.'

'Well, I suppose you can call Her that. Plus the Feast Day is December 4th, which is *our* Lilith's birthday.'

'Bar bar barbara,' they whispered, so as not to be heard by the little girl dancing outside.

'And she's patron saint of – listen to this – Artillerymen, Miners, Tunnellers, Prisoners, Mathematicians and *Chem-ic-al En-gin-eers*.'

She said that last in fragments, emphasising each syllable as if it was particularly significant.

When she was younger Gráinne had a reputation for clairvoyance. But there was also an aspect to her talent which eventually made her back off. Several times she wondered if she actually foresaw events for her clients, or if she was somehow making them happen. In fact she was so good that she rose like a helium balloon toward the lower reaches of the celebrity realm – such as it was then. Nowadays we'd think of them – if we even knew who they were - as B Listers.

But there was *always* an unforeseen consequence attached to the things that she brought about, even if they seemed brilliant at first. The more desperate the B Listers' hopes, the crueller the twists. Yet still they came. Which was one of the reasons why Gráinne blamed herself for Victoria sliding toward bad company and becoming the odious but newsworthy creature known as Slicky Vicky. She had wanted her unusual daughter to find fame and fortune – but not like that.

It was not that she had a switch that would turn on her clairvoyance. The most banal things could open up sudden vistas. These things sprang up, like gnosis from the soil. When she saw the term 'Chemical Engineers' then she was prickling all over, but without knowing why.

'Somehow this is connected with the Market Man isn't it?' asked Chazza, without turning from the mirror.

'Yes. I think we need to set a trap for him using Lilith. At the same Thursday Market, with all of us there.'

'Leave him to me.'

'We need to find out who or what is behind him.'

'Who is the most ruthless and unscrupulous? Who is likely to inflict most damage on him without us getting caught? Who is probably the best killer of all time?'

The answer to both of them was obvious. They answered in unison:

'Hope...'

In the eyes of the many men (staff and patients) in the sanatorium known as the Winsley Chest Hospital, Hope was... cute. A cross between a right little goer, and the sun, moon and stars – to the older, terminal ones. Her hair style and make-up changed from month to month. She seemed to keep apace with the latest, oddest fashions, as far as any young woman could in the depths of the West Country. She would come to work wearing hot-pants with platform shoes before changing into her uniform. Patients had been known to line the windows and applaud. She brought in magazines like Cosmopolitan and Vogue and bought tabloids like the News of the Screws and The Sun, and she didn't care who she shared Page 3 with.

Later decades would write her off as a bimbo, or air-head or (some rumours had it) prick-teaser. But she was sexy and innocently flirty with everyone, of *all* ages. She could reminisce with an octogenarian about the bad old good old days; all his systems might be failing, yet Hope could make him feel that she saw beyond the decrepitude to the Pure Man inside. Then he'd go to sleep remembering what it had been like to have known love.

She was always bubbly, cheerfully daft, did all the bed-changing and bottle-emptying or catheter-draining required of the untrained Nursing Auxiliary without complaint. Didn't get involved with ward or office politics, spoke to everyone the same, whether doctors, matrons or bin-men and was also, unknown to anyone except those in the final seconds of their lives, an Angel of Death.

A couple of her patients understood this and told her so.

'No, luvvy, I'm not *the* Angel of Death, I'm just *an* Angel of Death. There's a lot of us about you know!'

'Gizza kiss,' they'd invariably ask, and she did, and they smiled and sighed and closed their eyes.

When Hope was a young girl she had watched her mum dying in a cancer ward. One night, a very jolly lady came in and went from bed to bed, with a huge smile and a laugh. She was dressed all in black, vaguely nun-like but with the air of Father Christmas about her. She came to Hope's mum and her mum had opened her eyes wide as if she was meeting an old friend. For a moment, she was a young girl again. The nun-like woman put her hands on her hips and looked just like Oliver Hardy when he said *Another Fine Mess You've Got Us Into*. And Hope's mum did that thing with an invisible tie that Stan Laurel used to do. The pair of them laughed and then her mum died silently.

'Who are you?' Hope asked before the visitor disappeared.

'You already know that, my blossom. You're not quite of this world yourself.'

'Give me a name.'

'I'm an Angel of Death.'

'How can I learn what you've just done?'

'In the night-times, I will come and teach you. It's not hard.'

'Do I need to get angry, or inflict pain or hate people?'

'Noooooo! It's all about love, dearie.'

When Hope heard Granny and Chazza's plan, she couldn't wait to get stuck in...

Lily loved going to the various markets. When the others in the Sunday School heard that she actually helped run a stall, they were envious. They also heard that she rode on a goat in her garden, and that she had a tame owl. This wasn't a nasty envy, based on a perception of her being weirdly different; everyone wanted to be like her. A couple of them even got their parents to make them medals made out of budgie mirrors, like Lily sometimes wore. She enjoyed this sort of envy.

This time Granny actually had a proper stall, rather than some fold-out paste tables. It took a while to get all the pieces off the rack of the Land Rover and assembled, but her aunts were there to help. This one was like a little house with green and white stripes on the roof, and sides they could pull down if it rained.

'It won't rain, granny,' she assured.

The garden had been especially productive of late and when Faith looked toward her and said *I'm not surprised*, she knew what it meant but didn't say anything.

She spread out the vegetables and the fruit in her own way, biggest and heaviest near the front, all nicely patterned and not just dumped. Granny and her pals made no attempt to help and were more concerned with looking all around. Lily knew exactly who they were looking for but wasn't worried. She was a Market Trader, and that counted for more than anything.

Plus she had a dozen jars Plum, Strawberry, Raspberry and Greengage Jam that they had made together, and also several bottles of Granny's Scrumpy. That's exactly what it said on the label, hand written and stuck on with copydex. She understood that it was a powerful drink and that she must never ever sip it. In fact she had heard the word 'Scrumpy' before and seen the effects among some of her mummy's dreadful 'friends': the ones who would drink anything while injecting everything and completely ignoring her in her cot cage.

Her Aunty Hope had even bought her a special pinny with large pockets on the front to sort the change. Lily, the Market Trader, stood proudly behind her shiny fruit and robust veg and no-one ignored her. She decided that when she was Queen, she would make everyone come to these places. Indeed, in later life when she was fully into her covert power, she could still be glimpsed wandering happily through the various Farm Shops that became such a feature of the 21st Century. You probably passed her a dozen times without knowing. Indeed, a sort of myth sprang up that you can see Lilith's reflection in the sheen of an apple at such places, but you have to filter through that sort of thing yourself.

There was a vaguely awkward moment for Granny and the Guardians when Mr and Mrs Figge strolled by. Of course this was not accidental. Miriam had heard about Lily's stall from the other children in the class; Michael had hoped that Lily's aunt might be there.

'Hello!' they both said with feigned surprise.

Lily felt very proud. Being an Earthchild was brilliant. She knew the Big People were looking after the other side of her.

'Hello Lily,' said Mrs Figge.

'Hello Faith,' said Mr Figge.

The couple browsed the wares. They made silly noises for Lily's benefit. While Mrs Figge negotiated with Lily a bag of carrots and a punnet of late season strawberries, Faith picked up the juiciest apple and offered it to Mr Figge.

'It's a Cox,' she said softly. 'I do like Cox...'

The whole market might have seen the vicar's face burn red and his knees shake. Mrs Figge was too enamoured of the tiniest market trader to notice or care. She was happily paying ten times over the odds just to keep engaged: Lily looked so adorable putting the big silver coins in her apron pocket with serious intent.

More customers came and the Figges had to move on, with waves of bye-bye.

She is beautiful thought Mrs Figge looking at Lily.

She is beautiful thought Mr Figge looking at Faith.

'What a bitch you are Faith,' muttered Granny.

'Got to keep him on a leash, haven't we?'

Lilith knew all along where The Man was. She peeked out from Lily for a moment to tell Chazza:

'He's on the other side of the river. He's peeking out from the gates of the factory.'

She told Chazza because apparently Chazza liked a fight and even had a device in her handbag that she called a knuckleduster.

'Right,' said Chazza. 'Leave this to me and Hope. But save me some of that Scrumpy.'

'The Man', as he was thought of by Lilith's women, would never remember how he got to this spot. He was in the passenger seat of his own car on an isolated dirt road on a high hill with distant views of the chalk horses carved into the hillsides of Wiltshire.

'Oh hello Raymond!' said the chirpy girl with flame-red hair behind the wheel. 'Saw your name badge and stuff in your wallet: Raymond Pert. From Porton Down. Nice names.'

His head lolled back. This was in the years before head-rests were compulsory and his Renault 4 had none. He shouted in pain when a person behind him pushed it forward again. He glimpsed his own face in the rear-view mirror and saw the black eye and swollen lips. He felt as if he'd had ribs broken too, it was hard to breathe.

Had he been in a car crash?

The woman in the back had been at the market stall. She was wearing a brass knuckleduster and angling it to catch the light, like diamond rings.

'Please don't...'

'Actually I saved your life. You were beaten up by the guys in the Avon Rubber Factory when you tried to rape this sweet little thing behind the wheel. I had to pretend to be an off-duty policewoman and frog-marched you away. Then I thumped you a couple of times.'

'My friend's like that. Very physical. Oh, I'm Hope by the way. Nice little car.'

'Hope?'

'Everybody needs hope don't they? Really sweet little car. Can I have it?'

It hurt him to speak but: 'I need it.'

'No you won't,' from the back seat.

'What do you want?'

'The question is, what do you want? The stuff in your wallet says you work in Porton Down. What sort of place is that?'

'Can't say. Classified.'

'What?' asked Chazza. 'Speak up you moron!'

Hope sighed with exasperation.

'You broke his teeth you daft mare. I think poor Ray is trying to say *Classified. Cla-ssi-fied.* That right Ray? Sorry about grumpy in the back. Doesn't take much to give her the hump.'

'Look, you little shit, you might as well talk. You're going to die soon and no-one will find you for days. And do you know the worst of it? No-one in this Porton Down place will care. Within a day it will be as if you ne-ver ex-is-ted.'

It was true. No-one would. He had known that much about his colleagues for some time.

'Oh Ray Ray Ray, don't listen to that old meanie. *I* think you're lovely. Really. I do like the way you dress, proper respectable, neat and tidy. All the young guys chasing me now look like stupid girls, with their shoulder-length hair and earrings and flared trousers. Is that Brut you're wearing? Mmmm...'

His mind swirled. Hope was smiling. He'd never seen a nicer smile. She really seemed to like him. She even touched his sore face as if she would take away the pain. No woman had ever smiled at him like this. No woman had even touched his skin, other than doctors or dentists. He could tell that she was utterly sincere.

'I don't know much. I'm pretty low grade.'

'We can tell that from your car.'

'Oh shut up Chazza will you? It's a lovely car. Practical. Quirky. Like you, eh?'

Well yes, he *was* quirky. Inwardly. She was the only one who had ever seen that. The chaps in his department just thought he was a prick. The few women there didn't know he existed. Deep breath, then:

'Years ago, someone stole some new and highly-potent chemicals from a department that was also involved in some... unusual... experiments.'

'What sort of experiments, Ray?'

'As far as I was allowed to know, they had discovered how to pull things from the minds of certain people. With the help of this drug, they brought these things into real existence. Your worst nightmares now became real. Stalking the corridors. You wouldn't believe the stories I heard about that place.'

'I'd believe anything *you* told me Ray.'

'So why were you interested in Lilith?'

'I was told that her junkie mother was the one who had taken this drug and, after sex with an alien, conceived a monster. A particular kind of being, from very ancient times. Who will one day destroy us. Do you believe in monsters?'

Chazza sat back in her seat and laughed, thinking: *If only he knew...*

Hope did a *there there there* thing on all levels within the man.

'That wasn't so hard, was it? Thank you very *very* much Ray, and now you can stop worrying. As an old friend of mine might say: *Stuff and nonsense.*'

'They suspect that your Lilith is a particular kind of monster. It's not nonsense, its -'

'Ssshh...'

So he *ssshd*. In fact he was so tired he just wanted to sleep. Hope's perfect face peered at him like that of an angel from a cloud. Her cool hands with scarlet nails held onto his, her thumbs stroking against his knuckles.

'Who do you miss most in all the world, Ray? I know how lonely you are.'

'Mummy,' he said at once.

'Oh that is so cute. You really are special Ray, and you've done your best for your country - probably more than anyone will ever know.'

'True. Thank you.'

'But hey, look - look down there!'

He strained forward in his seat. He peered through his swollen eyes down the empty road.

'It's mummy,' he whispered in astonishment.

'Go to her, Ray. Can't you see her waving?'

'Yes. Yes. Sorry for what I did.'

'Forgiven.'

'Thank you for finding mummy.'

'You're welcome.'

'Please may I go to her?'

'You may. Go and find peace.'

'Thank you.'

Before he died, simply by slumping in the seat when his soul left his body, he took one last look at the shining woman who was making this possible. Her smile was gorgeous. She was stunning. He was deeply in love. In the softest of voices he asked:

'You're a monster too, aren't you?'

The evenings were drawing in, the nights getting colder. They did her a hot water bottle and made sure Lily was nicely tucked up in bed after getting stories from her aunts. They were all childless; they loved doing this.

Faith read her bits of *Fantastic Mr Fox* with all the voices.

Hope read *The Little Match Girl* and cried.

Chazza did *Where the Wilds Things Are,* and hoped that Lily might filter through to Lilith something about transformations and anger and loneliness.

Downstairs, when they were sure she was curled on her side asleep and cuddling the teddy, they toasted each other with small glasses of cider.

'I should have realised it was Porton Down,' said Gráinne .

'What is the place? The sense I got from Ray before I released him wasn't very nice.'

'Here, offered Chazza. 'I returned the book on saints and borrowed this one on local history.'

'Same armpit?'

'The other one. This is smaller. Listen...'

So they listened while Chazza read about Porton Down being known as the Microbiological Research Establishment, dealing with exotic viruses and biological warfare.

'That's the Chemical Engineers of Saint Barbara.'

'Well I should have known that too,' said Chazza. 'I had a beau once, sort of, who worked for MI5.'

'Your Waggo?'

'Yep, Colonel Waghorn. Y'know I can't remember his first name. Strange bod, involved in all sorts of shifty things. Apparently, to keep up with the Yanks and Russkis, they formed a department which experimented with what he called 'remote viewing'. Anyway, as for Porton, he let slip that numbers of innocent folk, servicemen, were tricked into applying for a few weeks at the place for research into the common cold. Yet they were injected with all sorts of things, ranging from that LSD they all talk about – that your Vicky stole – and the nerve agent Sarin.'

'Manifesting monsters?'

'Never mentioned them, Faith. Probably beyond his pay-scale. I think he was actually outraged that soldiers had survived the War and yet were being murdered by their own country, which is why he babbled – slightly.'

'Monsters…bah! sounds like the sort of things my ectoplasmic great-granny would show to Arthur Conan Doyle down the Old Kent Road.'

'We have to go there.'

'Through the mirror?'

'How else?'

Today, anyone can go on-line and learn about the secret places that all civilised nations have, wherein the most uncivilised acts have been committed. Over the years these have also been connected with extra-terrestrials, star people, or simple grey aliens, depending on fashion – which changes as frequently as Hope's hairstyles. And very often they blend these in with the Illuminati, the shape-shifting Lizard Kings, Shadow Governments and all manner of Black Projects involving anti-gravity and time travel that would cause any normal citizen to revolt if they knew how their tax money was being spent. In Britain there is Rudloe Manor, Porton Down, RAF Bentwaters and Chicksands, and for over a year a little air force base near Weston super Mare, plus dozens of other truly secret places scattered across the land like acupuncture points.

It is not the locales that are significant, as the fact that there are places within the psyches of governments that hide things, as the Moon itself hides its far side. After all, governments are only formed from bumbling humans, none of them much brighter than Vicar Figge: they have to conceal their secrets somewhere, somehow. Not unlike Granny and the Guardians hiding Lilith's feet.

Given their uncanny natures it was a simple task for the four women to peer at their country's hidden far side. They took the large mirror from the wall, turned it around and placed it on the floor. They did things with that simple glass that Lilith somehow did with the telly. They sat around it by firelight, watching the images build.

They had all, in their differing ways, done this sort of scrying many a time. In fact this was how Granny kept track of her daughter when Victoria did everything she could to avoid her mother. She had even been present in vision that night when her daughter seduced a very odd and not entirely human little man who was Lilith Mary's father. It was hardly surprising that her daughter was often accused of being paranoid in those years: she really *was* being watched. She could almost hear her mother *tut tutting* down through the planes.

What did they see that night?

They saw terrible things that were – in the minds of some - done for the good of the nation. They saw good things that might have awful consequences further down the time-lines. The inner doings of Porton Down and its sinister aspects were of no particular concern to Gráinne and pals. They only wanted to know if there was anything there, on the surface or deep down within the top-secret laboratories, that might threaten Lilith and that little girl's own especial mission.

And when they had seen all that the mirror would allow then they picked it up, turned it back onto the wall, looked at each other in silence and gave a collective:

Ooooh...

If the little girls and boys in the children's books had midnight feasts or made secret forest dens or rafts to float down rivers without the adults knowing, then the girl upstairs had her own agenda. She was fully aware that Granny and Co. were doing things downstairs. Behind their backs, feeling little-girl-naughty and rather pleased, Lilith put on her wings and flew.

What did *she* see that night?

She flew up and down and in and out of the dimensions and planes that impinge upon us all, without our knowing. Granny would have had a fit if she glimpsed the depths (or heights) that she was exploring: planes of existence layered upon each other like rock strata; dimensions beyond the fourth that no human could possibly explain. She saw the earthbound spirits of the valley, from the Stone Age, through to the Ancient Brits and Celts and Romans and Angles and Saxons and Danes. Danes particularly, in that area. Some of them she released, and she seemed to have always known how to do this; others were little more than echoing shells doing no-one any harm so she let them continue to haunt the land. And she saw the beings that some would call the Sylphs, Gnomes, Salamanders and Undines of the Elemental Kingdoms and clapped when they all danced for her, as if she were their long-lost oldest friend. Then she saw the Lordly Ones – the tall, slim, shining souls that some would call the Sidhe. And she saw Earth Giants from the depths that had no modern name or awareness, and Star Beings that could adapt to all sorts of shapes and appear as how you needed.

It was Granny's jigsaw again. She had no desire to fit it all together and make sense of the parallel worlds within her valley. It was multi-spiritual, chaotic, marvellous, scary, rhapsodic. The silvery, rippling energies flowed along and through it like the River Avon at its base.

Ooooh... she thought, but in a different way to that uttered by the ladies downstairs.

This became a nightly jaunt. Sometimes, when she sank into reverie as Lily, she could access it during daytime as well. Granny and the others knew she was doing this. Once, at Sunday School, she saw a little boy hiding from his mum behind a box, when she came to pick him up. He thought that if he couldn't see *her*, then she couldn't see *him*, despite his legs sticking out. Lilith felt a bit like that with her protectors. They all thought it rather sweet, and Lilith allowed Lily savour this. Only once, when Lilith was confronting very strange and hostile energies that shaped as dragons, did she become aware of Granny right behind her, driving the creatures away.

They think they rule the world, that lot, came Granny's thoughts on the matter before they both flew back into their bodies.

If Granny was able to walk out into the garden every morning and fit into the rhythms of the land, Lilith would one day do the same for the inner realms. If Lilith's presence in Dicky Bird House somehow gave the vegetables a particular boost, then she would have a similar effect on the whole area on more subtle levels.

The land has its own patterns and flows, growth and decay. So every region has moments when there are more phenomena than usual. The people then experience plagues of crop circles, UFO's, plasma lights, Shadow People, Black Eyed Kids, poltergeists or phantom hitch-hikers - the whole gamut of supernatural manifestations. Then they disappear and become no more than charming local myths and legends.

In Canada and the U.S. people today glimpse Bigfoot; in England, giant Black Dogs or even Cats. The egregores aren't 'real' in the physical realms: you will never catch them with bear traps or infra-red cameras. To find these 'monsters' you will need to find the person in the area who is acting like a generator. Cases of poltergeist disturbance are always linked to one person within the building who somehow magnifies the hidden energies. Usually a pre-pubescent girl. If a small, pre-pubescent girl could unleash that sort of thing within a house, imagine the effect that a Lilith might have upon a landscape...

There was a time when the small town of Warminster was regarded – usually tongue-in-cheek – as a hot-spot for transgalactic visitors. Others talked about the Thing that stopped cars in their tracks, killed birds, terrified children and sparked reports of strange humming noises, tremors, lights, crop circles, UFOs, and even alien abductions.

It was in all the national and international newspapers and people came from far and wide to experience the wonders. Ernest folk kept vigils on the nearby hills and wrote books. Some associated it with either the end of the world or the Second Coming. Some of the ones on the hills, writing books, claimed *they* were the Second Coming, though no-one followed them and the world never ended. The Ministry of Defence denied it was anything to do with their top-secret work in the nearby military bases. As was said at the time: *Well they would, wouldn't they?*

None of them could have guessed that it was all triggered off because a little girl came to sell fruit and veg at the Warminster Market with her Granny every Friday, thereby unleashing all kinds of unsettling events.

Nearer home, despite the best efforts of the Guardians, this also affected the entire length and breadth of the Limpley Stoke valley and surrounding hills that were Lilith's habitat. Locals whispered cautiously at first, then more openly, when they spoke about a winged humanoid that they had glimpsed in the valley at night. It was...

perched in a tree
hooting with an owl
flying across the Moon
hovering above my greenhouse
the dogs went mad!
it just sank into the ground
it just rose from the ground
the wings were black
the wings were silver
it had the cruellest eyes
feet like claws

hands like talons

The members of the Mah-jong, Bridge and Canasta clubs made sure they got home before dark. At the other extreme The Seven Stars sold large quantities of Real Ale and microwaved pies to the excitable punters who wanted to see the Winged Devil of Winsley Hill.

Vicar Figge was consulted. He had no idea what to do, but would never confess that. He put it down to mass hysteria and said clever things about the Devils of Loudun, but that satisfied no-one. *That* was psychological fiction: *this* was real. Dismayed by his parishioners' scorn, he promised to consult higher powers, by which he meant his bishop.

Mrs Figge, who had a greater belief in the otherworld than her husband, was deeply worried for Lily. She imagined her being snatched, abducted, vampirised and lay awake at night visualising stories in which she rescued the little girl from all manner of evil. She re-awakened her own faith, like pulling an old war-time pistol from beneath the bed, in the belief that she had to find a weapon – however rusty - to protect Lily.

Once, at Sunday School, when all the others were doing potato stamps, she pulled Lily aside and discharged the first round from her old weapon. She whispered to her Psalm 91: 5-7 and it felt like she had fired a shot into the air to give notice to any Malignities that *this* little child was under her protection, and that They would get the next one right between their evil eyes…

> *You will not fear the terror of night,*
> *nor the arrow that flies by day,*
> *nor the pestilence that stalks in the darkness,*
> *nor the plague that destroys at midday.*
> *A thousand may fall at your side,*
> *ten thousand at your right hand,*
> *but it will not come near **you**, Lily…*

'Thank you,' said Lily, who was actually the Malignity in question, but who was enjoying cutting the potatoes Granny had provided in half, then carving shapes, then dabbing the shapes into poster paint and stamping patterns.

Miriam Figge surged with love and thanked Jesus.

Her husband passed by. Her husband, she thought, looked haunted. She didn't care.

'My word, Lily... they are splendid patterns,' he said. 'They look like cuneiform writing from Ancient Sumer!'

Prick thought his wife.

'Sorry,' said Lily, who knew exactly what she was carving.

The vicar moved on, trailing big anxieties and small farts. The class continued until the Big People came to take their children home, while keeping their eyes on the lowering skies and dark places amid the woods.

They imagined satanic sacrifices and black masses, though few of them could have said what, exactly, a *white* mass might have involved. Reporters from *The Sun* turned up, followed by Maxy Mack of the *News of the World*. There were rumours that *The National Enquirer* was going to send someone from the States. The locals found there was money to be made from their yarns: sightings of the winged humanoid quadrupled.

'Is that your Vicky showing her tits on page 3 of *The Sun*?' asked Hope, amid all of this nonsense. 'Nice pair...'

'She was boasting about her threesome with the Thin White Duke and his wife in last week's issue,' added Faith. 'Lucky for some, eh?'

'We've got to stop this,' sighed Gráinne, watching Lilith on her tricycle, singing her favourite nursery rhyme *How Many Miles to Babylon* as she zoomed back and forth along the garden paths:

How many miles to Babylon?
Three score miles and ten.
Can I get there by candle-light?
Yes, and back again.

'What's the greatest threat? The monster-makers at Porton, or Lilith's night-time adventures?'

'I'm not sure, Chaz. I suspect that Ray was just a loose cannon. I think he was seeking redemption for having given that special stuff to Victoria in the first place in return for a quickie. His fault. And he bigged up what They were doing to scare us.'

'We did glimpse someone connected with wires to his brain and all sorts of electronic dials and thingamajigs.'

'I know.'

'And although we only saw him from behind, and the clear space in front that might manifest his 'monsters', you do know who we thought it was, don't you?'

'I know, Faith. You didn't want to upset me. It did look like Zak.'

Hmmmm... they said in unison, staring out through the net curtains and into the garden.

While they were saying that, Vicar Michael Figge was searching for his own solution to this problem of black magic on his hill. For once, for a short time, he put aside his overwhelming thoughts about Faith and made a few phone calls. The notion of Six Degrees of Separation was as true then as it is now, but within a mere four calls he had found a man who might take some of the pressure off himself. He confessed as much to Faith when she turned up for her cleaning.

'My goodness, Mr. Figge,' she said before he opened his mouth. 'This place is an absolute tip today! It'll take me more time to get sorted, if that's okay? I won't charge you extra.'

'That's perfectly agreeable, ma cherie. But do call me Michael. I *will* pay you the extra.' He didn't confess that *he* had created the extra mess to keep her there longer.

She assembled her hoover and various mops, pulled on her pinny. He had never seen anyone so graceful, so lovely and yet again tried not to stare. The emotions he felt for her were like the Flood itself, sweeping away most of his known world. He decided to impress her, and also extend his spiritual protection during these dark and queasy times:

'I'm bringing someone to help us deal with the evil that seems to stalk our little world.'

'Oh! Who?'

'Let me look in the Clerical Directory,' he said, moving to his desk and browsing through the large tome, not wearing his usual cardigan so that if her perfect breast touched his shoulders again as she peered over, then he would get more sensation. He felt wicked; he felt clever as Satan when her breast did exactly that. He took some time turning the pages to the section beginning 'O'.

'Oh. Oh. *Om*and,' he almost stuttered, shaking slightly. 'The Reverend Dr. Donald Omand.'

'Who is he?' asked Faith, moving her other breast to touch him, her sweet breath so close to his face that he turned quickly to kiss her, seizing the moment, the *carpe diem* thing that he had never done.

She stood back, all sweet innocence, no contact made. They faced each other, he didn't know what to do.

'Well?'

Then after an infinitely long pause in which he assessed all possibility of meanings for that single word, he answered:

'He's an exorcist. That's Latin. It means someone who can drive out evil spirits.'

Prick thought Faith, who was beginning to weary of being patronised but still kept smiling.

'He's coming to exorcise the whole hill and valley...'

But thou art beyond man and woman, my star is
in thee, and thou shalt avail
The Book of Babalon

The Reverend Dr. Donald Omand was never shy of publicity. Among other things he was known as the Circus Padre, exorcizing men and beasts alike, often getting into the cage with troubled lions because his rites would never have worked through the bars, he felt. In his time he travelled all over Europe at the request of fellow priests, medical doctors, psychiatrists and troubled villagers.

A modest, respectful man, he did like publicity. He was quite happy to be known as the vicar who exorcised the monstrous Black Dog of Kettleness, near Whitby, the entirety of the Bermuda Triangle and had spent a cold, grey morning ridding the world of the Loch Ness Monster. For which act Gráinne and Co were rather inclined to curse him.

'Poor wee beastie,' muttered Faith, drawing on her Scottish roots.

As for the Bermuda Triangle, then Gráinne did her usual:

'Stuff **AND** Nonsense! There is NO. SUCH. THING.'

'Oh this is such fun,' chimed Hope. 'Shall we go and watch?'

Chazza had other ideas.

'I think we should stop him.'

'With your knuckleduster?'

'No, no, but we must be ready to do our own thing in case he might be able to sense our little girl.'

'Oh come on, Chaz, she is far *far* beyond any sensing that *he* might be able to manage. But I do think you three should go and watch. I'll keep Lilith busy in the garden, and then making more jam. She loves that. That'll keep her busy and grounded.'

'Just watch?'

'Yes. Chaz. I actually think he might be part of the solution to our problems. He'll persuade everyone that the hill and valley are purified, and that the disturbances will end. And then... And then we'll sit down with Lilith and give her The Talk.'

'About the Birds and the Bees, you mean? It's another 10 years before her periods start!'

'No, Faith. About the Anunnaki...'

A large crowd had gathered in an empty field near the Hartley Farm, which was recognised to be the highest point of Winsley Hill and the centre of its landmass. Vicar Figge was notable by his absence. He did not want his bishop to associate him with this circus, or blame him if it went nasty.

The Reverend Dr. Donald Omand arrived in a red sports car along with his aide, who gave his name to the watching journalists as Captain Tony Artus, a serving artillery officer.

'Are you *confirmed* bachelors, gentlemen?' asked Maxy Mack from the *News of the World* - a query that was lost on the people around but which drew icy glares from the two men concerned.

The exorcist was a jolly looking fellow: chubby, white haired, cheerful. With an almost child-like air about him, as if he was about to go on a bouncy castle rather than drive out demons from the Pit.

'If we can just hang on three minutes, my friends. Those people crossing the field now are from the BBC and they'll need a moment to get their equipment in order.'

The great and good shuffled positions like they did cards in Canasta. Even then, on the brink of the 1970s, some people would do a lot to get on the telly. And there was no higher consecrated act in their minds than being on the BBC.

When the press and cameramen were all ready the Reverend Dr. Donald Omand asked everyone to kneel or at least bow their heads while he went around the group making the sign of the cross and sprinkling holy water.

'You are now protected!' he cried, in rather a powerful voice.

I'm on the pill, whispered Faith from the back row.

I use Durex, said Hope.

I'd rather have a cocoa, from Chazza.

Then the Reverend Dr. Donald Omand prayed, and prayed hard:

'Grant that by the power entrusted to Thy unworthy servant, this hill and the valley adjoining it may be delivered from the wingèd demon and all its attendant evil spirits...'

Shall we give him a storm?

Okay Faith, you do the wind. Hope, start the thunder and rain.

No rain! I've just had a perm.

Okay, then I'll do the lightning.

Can you still do lightning?

Is the Pope a Catholic or the Duke of Edinburgh a giant Lizard!?

At the centre of all this the Reverend Dr. Donald Omand took it onto another level:

'Deliver us from all vain imaginations; projections and phantasms; and all deceits of the evil one!'

A strong wind sprang up from the west, bringing billowing clouds. The sky darkened. The thunder began, a distant rolling at first but coming closer by the second.

The Reverend Dr. Donald Omand saw all this and loved it. This was proof that what he did was real!

'O Lord, subject the demons and their wingèd leader to Thy servant's commands that, at his bidding, they will harm neither man nor beast, but depart to the place appointed them, there to remain forever.'

The whole of the hilltop seemed to explode as lightnings crashed all around and the congregation, as it was, screamed but stayed put within the vicar's cheerful protection.

You've still got it, Chazza.

They can still have it!

Let's stop it now though.

'Peace be still!' the Reverend Dr. Donald Omand cried at the last with every fibre of his being and the thunder and lightning stopped, the wind died completely and the clouds dissolved like smoke.

It became still.

The people were impressed. The journalists and the BBC team felt they had scoops and all raced off to beat their rivals. The erstwhile congregation of the haunted, possessed and merely curious gave the Reverend Dr. Donald Omand a round of applause.

Wish our vicar was like this, was the general mutter.

As the three guardians linked arms and headed back toward the village and thence down into the valley, they were stopped by Reverend Dr. Donald Omand's companion.

'You three didn't take this seriously,' he mused, looking at Hope and her mini-skirt and bra-less t-shirt with interest. 'You three are not what you seem.'

'We're all confirmed spinsters, mein Kapitän,' said Chazza with a salute. 'No good sniffing around us.'

'That's not what I mean.'

They walked on with a quicker step and took the long way back to Dicky Bird House, making sure they weren't followed.

In the event, to the utter frustration of all concerned, not a single photograph taken by any of the journalists was usable, and even the camera of the BBC showed nothing but a grey fuzz with what might have been a very blurry, large, dark hairy-headed person-shape in the distance, amid the trees. Asked for his comment the Reverend Dr. Donald Omand said that he was not surprised, that it was a testimony to the maleficent power of the creature he had banished. He was more than happy to robe up and have a mock ceremony in his back garden if they wanted to photograph and use that. No-one would know the difference, he added chirpily.

'Now Lilith, you've got a lot of people frightened,' said Gráinne, cuddling her tight before the fire, with the curtains closed and winter's cold surrounding the house.

'Sorry Granny.'

'Don't be sorry. You are very special and very powerful, but you know that don't you?'

'Yes.'

'Now for the next few years we've really got to keep you hidden.'

'Don't send me away.'

'What? Never! Stuff and *Nonsense*! This valley would crush me with an avalanche if I did that. Or Owl, Snake and Goat would eat me alive. I even think your tricycle might run me over.'

Lilith smiled at the thought. 'Can I have a bicycle now?'

'Ask Aunty Chazza about that!'

She wrapped her up tight in a furry blanket, cuddled her again and they both sighed with delight.

'I've got to try and explain who you are.'

'Thank you.'

Gráinne had two mirrors, one in each hand. She manoeuvred them at either side of Lilith's head.

'I was taught this by someone called The Merlin. That's a title. Every area has one, though no-one knows. Sometimes even *they* don't know! He's not one of us, but he's also not ordinary. We *never* mix. Oil and water. Ours lives in Limpley Stoke. He's a bit pompous.'

'Big hairy man. Nice suit, beard.'

'Erm yes, you've seen him? When you fly? When you travel?'

'He was on the top of the hill today, hiding in the woods with his black dog, watching the silly man with the white collar.'

'I thought you were concentrating on the jam making!'

'Sorry. The silly man was shouting about me, so I thought I'd peek in my budgie mirror.'

'Little toad.'

'Thank you Granny.'

'Look...'

Lilith saw an endless line of Liliths reflected in the glass.

'Now imagine – just imagine – that everyone of those little girls there had a slightly different life to yours. With a slightly different beginning and ending. They are called parallel lives. Par-a-llel.'

'Do you understand?

'Yes Granny,' she yawned, as if this was something she had always known, and snuggled further into the thick blanket. She loved the feel of warmth on her bare feet from the fireplace.

'But we have to see where the very first Lilith came from, and the only way I can do that is by making you into teeny, tiny Starchild and taking you back there.'

'Can I still have a bicycle?'

Gráinne had always had a phrase at the back of her mind that declaimed: 'I am a child of Earth, but my race is of the starry Heavens.' She had long since forgotten where she had first heard this. Perhaps it was something that Zak had quoted when he tried to get her involved in a UFO-ey religion of the time, the Aetherius Society. 'Gráinne,' he had whined, 'there is more evidence for UFOs than there is for God.'

'Stuff and Nonsense,' she had said, and also added 'Tosh!' on that occasion. She knew as well as anyone that there were any number of alien beings mingling on Planet Earth, and not all of them were friendly.

Now that they had glimpsed Zak in Porton Down, however, she would have to completely revise her attitude toward that man. To be able to hide that side of himself from herself and the Aunts meant that there was more to him, and more power, than met the eye. She might get Chazza to ask him a few pointed questions.

In the meantime though, Lilith's Starchild education was even more necessary than that of being a Moonchild or an Earthchild...

In those years when the US (using rocket propulsion technology that was pioneered by Jack Parsons), used their monstrous Saturn V beasts to send men to the Moon, and even managed to send an unmanned Mariner 9 to Mars, Granny and Lilith went light years beyond them from a bedroom in Dicky Bird House.

Leaving their bodies was easy-peasy and they looked down upon themselves as they lay side by side in Granny's big bed.

'Lilith, you can become big - big as the planet - but there will be someone to see you. That's what's been happening lately when you've whizzed up and down the valley and around the hill. It's like saying to people, *Look at me!* And some of them *do* see, and none of them understand.'

'Like Vicar Figge.'

'Well yes, but he will be harmless. Aunty Faith will see to that.'

'She will break his heart.'

'Oh that's a very grown up thing to say!'

'I saw it on Sooty and Sweep.'

'Hmm, well, there are worse things. Some people never get to know that sort of thing. But are we going to explore the stars or not?'

'Izzy wizzy let's get busy...'

'You see, Lilith, not many people, in thousands and thousands of years have been able to understand the very first Lilith, who started off all those parallel lives.'

130

'Sorry Granny.'

'No, don't say that! You have to learn! And I know how much fun it is. But now we're going to become very very small. Smaller than your budgie mirror. If anyone see us they'll just see two lights in the sky, like shooting stars. We have to go to the stars now.'

In the nights that followed, depending upon Lilith's contact with her far side, there were moments when Granny was very much the junior partner. When she tried to introduce Lilith to the Beings out beyond our galaxy it was sometimes clear that her ancient self already knew some of them.

It was never a matter of going toward planets that had material structures such as space-ports: it was all about getting into frequencies of light and thereby creating meeting points. Some people might visualise these as temples, others as unearthly landscapes. To Lilith and Granny, these were simply places within their heads in which they could approach particular stars and say Hello!

'Remember Lilith, it is all within. It's not about spaceships. What's it NOT about?'

'Spaceships, Granny.'

'Now listen, before we start, I'm about to have a rant. This will mean nothing to you now but when the time comes apply what I tell you in the future, when I'm not here. You're good at remembering aren't you?'

'Yes granny. I never forget.'

'The three stars in Orion's Belt do NOT align exactly with the pyramids. One of them is slightly out. The pyramids align EXACTLY with a certain three stars in the constellation of Cygnus. In fact we'll zoom up there to the Great Rift and you can see for yourself and meet the Swan People. They are waiting for you. And they're not the only ones. And yes, yes, you can have a ruddy bicycle.'

'Okay Granny.'

So they went toward Cygnus and they saw the bird-faced people on that distant world with its buildings made of blood red stone and two suns in the pale sky above the turquoise lagoons. She met tall, spindly women with dark, reddish brown skin and high pointy breasts. Their legs and arms were long, as were their fingers. Their feet were encased in elegant sandals with turned-up toes that looked like they were covered by golden foil. They had head coverings not unlike tea-towels, that encircled the head above the eyes and hung down in back and the sides, to the bony shoulders.

Lilith wanted sandals like that.

They like me, she said to Granny in her mind.

Of course they do! When you think about it, birds don't judge. And your pal Owl – and all his pals - will fly to someone with a severe disability, giving that person a sense of equality.

They stayed in that timeless zone for some time. Lilith learned all sorts of things that would be very hard to explain and she understood why the swans at Bradford on Avon's market had protected her, as she would always protect them.

After coming back to Dicky Bird House again they lay cuddling, remembering, comparing notes. It was dark outside, 7 o'clock, long after a little girl's usual bedtime. But this was not a usual little girl.

'And then there is Sirius. Nice beings around there. Let's go. In Egypt, where I'll take you some day, they associated the rising of Sirius with a lady called Isis. But modern folk, viewing from the Northern hemisphere, said that her brother Osiris was to be seen in the huge, adjoining constellation of Orion. The **stupidity**! The mighty Isis trotting along after Orion like a little puppy! And no **you** can't have a puppy! If they went toward the Southern hemisphere they'd see that Sirius matches and perfectly dances with the star known as Canopus. **Ca-no-pus,** the second-brightest star in the night-time sky, after Sirius. We'll go and see that, too. Canopus is where you meet Osiris – if you ever need to. Personally I find him rather boring. Come on, teeny tiny again...'

Lilith learned that 'Sirian' covered as many differing types of Being as, say, 'Asian' could express on earth. The ones she met on her first encounter with Granny were elegant beings with lovely deep, dark oval eyes and fingers as long as the Swan Ladies.

We've had a few at our Warminster Market stall over the weeks. They weren't after the apples. They came to peek at **you**.

I know, Granny.

I thought you did. Well, there's too much to experience in one go and you'll come back to Sirius again in your own time. So let's go home now. Tomorrow night we'll go to...

'The Pleiades. It looks like the eye of the constellation known as Taurus. There are Seven Sisters up there – which is really in your funny little head here – who can't wait to say Hello! Their names are-'

'Maya, Electra, Alkyone, Taygety, Asteropy, Celeno and Meropy.'

'Ow! You didn't get *that* from *Sooty and Sweep,* or *The Clangers.'*

'I see them when I sit on the Hump in our garden.'

'That's understandable.'

'They look like you and my aunties.'

'Well, we are just reflections, as I explained before.'

'Where are the other three?'

'Oh they're around somewhere. They'll turn up unexpectedly if we ever need them. They're probably keeping an eye on your mum.'

As soon as Gráinne said that she could have bit her tongue, because the small child known as Lily made a sudden, sad appearance.

'I never hear from her. She must be busy; she's the best mum in the world.'

Granny tried not to sigh; tried not to give anything away. It was much easier up within the stars than down upon the earth.

Izzy wizzy let's get busy. Come on, let's go, she said with her mind – and so they went...

Over the weeks, Lilith spent as much time exploring the stars as she did digging into the earth around Dicky Bird House. When she was into the far side of her Moonchild self, she could have stayed forever. When the light shifted, she was quite happy to be Lily again, with all of the concerns a safe and loved little girl might have. What *Lilith* learned could have filled dozens of thick tomes of the sort that were even then, at the start of the 70s, beginning to make bookshelves groan. But Lilith didn't want that. If it couldn't be said quickly and simply, backed up by silent presence, then she wasn't interested.

When Granny told her the story of Who she was and Where she came from, she was happy for it to be in the form of a fairy-tale…

Once before a Time there were some people who came from a far-away world called Nibiru and settled in a place called Sumer. They called themselves the Anunnaki.

There was Enki who was a good person, although he often did wrong things. And his twin brother En-Lil who could be nasty if you didn't obey his rules. Enki needed some help on Earth so he created what we now call People. He did so by splicing bits of himself, like Granny does with plants, then injecting bits of himself into them. He was very pleased with the result and he called the first person he created The Adam.

Enki was married to Lilith who was said to be a Dragon Queen who could tame all beasts.

In time, the very first members of the Anunnaki who came to this world came to realise that they had done silly things and felt guilty. So their mum, Nammu, sent echoes of themselves into the present day to put things right. She appeared herself in the shape of Sister Ndlovu.

Granny told the tale as simply as she could. Lilith listened as attentively as she cared. In truth – if there *is* such a thing – the story meant no more to her than those of Mary, Mungo and Midge, or the lively doings of Sooty, Sweep and Soo. She really wasn't interested in the events on this world a million years after the dinosaurs or how her Granny and her Aunts knew about all this. She was far more interested in the Now.

'They are very guilty about the mess They made,' finished Granny with her tale. 'That's why you have been sent...'

'Sorry Granny,' she said, putting her thumb into her mouth and snuggling in.

One week in November Lilith experienced something far more amazing than anything she had yet known in the Milky Way. This was the week she made a human friend.

She arrived at Sunday School as usual with Granny dropping her off this time. The mood from Mrs Figge was grim.

'Children children children' she intoned. 'I have some very bad news. Our little classmate Maisy is seriously ill in hospital. She is very *very* poorly.'

Lily was aware of Maisy, who had kept to herself and did clumsy drawings in the corner of the room and spoke so quietly because of a speech impediment that no-one else could hear. But she had never tried to engage with her or indeed any of the others in the class. Maisy had what was then known by the crude term 'Mongolism', and it would be a few years yet before this was changed to the softer Downs Syndrome. To Lily, she just had rather unusual eyes, but she'd seen enough varieties of these among the various Star Beings not to ask questions.

Lilith had a sudden new feeling within herself. And it was not pleasant. When Granny had told her about the Anunnaki there had one bit she never understood. It was the feeling of guilt, which surged through her now.

Here was Maisy, a harmless little girl her own age who was neglected and rejected by the others, just as she had been within the Children's Home in London. And neither Lily nor Lilith had done anything about it.

'Children, children, I want us all to get into a circle and bow our heads and clasp our hands to pray for her, ' said Mrs Figge on the verge of tears. 'She is not expected to live.'

So they all did, and Lily joined in (which wasn't usual for her). Mrs Figge called upon Jesus and Saint Barbara and a few others including God. They all finished with a big *Amen*, although Lily whispered *Nine Moons*. No-one wanted milk and biscuits. Everyone was subdued when they went home. The Big People on the hill who knew of Maisy made all the expected noises; many of whispered that it was for the best. Maisy's unmarried, jobless mum was old when she had had her, and the father had run off, leaving them in a small council flat at the edge of the village. Mongols had congenital health problems that would only get worse. Mongols never lived long, anyway. Mongols could never live a full life and they should be aborted in future. It was for the best. They all agreed.

All of this completely passed Gráinne by. When she had picked Lily up from the Sunday School and asked her what she'd been doing, the only reply was a brief 'Nothing', before she went out to talk to Owl. Granny just wasn't in touch with local gossip. But she *was* surprised the next day when she saw Maisy's Mum and Maisy making their way down the path to Dicky Bird House. It was frosty, the ground was silver, the land was silent, there was still a crescent moon in a white sky.

136

Without a word, Lily went and held Maisy's hand and took off her to see Goat. The pair of them were wearing little duffel coats: Maisy's red, Lily's blue. With their hoods up on the cold day, they looked like mini-priestesses from an ancient cult.

The two women stared at each. Both had the sense that something very unusual had happened, neither knowing what, or even what to say. Maisy's mum began, almost declaiming:

'Yesterday morning at 11, Maisy was in hospital with sepsis. The doctors told me that there was nothing they could do any more, that it was too late. They drew curtains around the bed so that I could give her final cuddles.'

'I didn't know that, sorry.'

'Then your Lily slid between the curtains and climbed up on the chair to be next to Maisy.'

'She couldn't have done. She was at Sunday School. I took her there and picked up her up.'

'I'm telling you, Lily slid between the curtains and climbed up on the chair and then held Maisy's hand.'

'Really, she couldn't have been there.'

'She climbed up on the chair and held Maisy's hand and said *Time is*, and after some flickering, Maisy's eyes opened. And Maisy smiled. And...and.. I'm sorry if I'm crying but...but...'

'I'm crying too!'

'And then the dark patches on her skin faded, as they held hands... sorry...sorry... Maisy was... Maisy was cured.'

'Oh Maisy's Mum I am so *happy* for you both! But... Lily couldn't be in two places at the same time.'

Actually, in her later life, Lilith was to be noted by many others for somehow being in two places at the same time. Yet she couldn't have explained it either. In the madness of quantum mechanics, where modern versions of Enki insist that teeny-tiny particles can exist in two separate locations at once, she still would never analyse it beyond saying *Time Is*, and moving along.

137

'Listen, I ripped aside the curtains and shouted for the nurses and when they came they were all amazed. There was no sign of Lily. I asked where she had gone, or if you were with her, but no-one had passed by the nurses' station. We were alone. There was no dark-haired little girl. They thought I might have been hallucinating with the stress, but I didn't care and said nothing more. Maisy was well. And she said to pass this on to you...'

She held out the budgie-mirror. It was Lilith's own, the original that other children copied. Granny took it very carefully, as if it might break.

'I don't know what to say.'

'Don't. I will say nothing to anyone about your Lily. I know there is something special about her – and you. If anyone asks, I'll say they gave Maisy some new antibiotics.'

'Thank you.'

'Maisy's real name is Ava, you know. After the film star Ava Gardner. But she always wanted to be called Maisy after the *Maisy Mouse* books.'

'Oh Lily loves them too. But her name is really Lilith. Lilith Mary. Her mum named her after the Mother of Nightmares *and* the Mother of God. Though we keep that a secret!'

'Look, look at them, riding on the goat! They're laughing! Isn't that the most beautiful sight in the whole universe?'

Gráinne, who had been to places where she had seen worlds colliding and stars being born, heard the little girls' laughter echoing across the valley and had to agree.

'It is, it really is.'

So Maisy met Goat, Owl and Snake while the two Big People stood at the edge of the vegetable patches and watched.

'Whatever it is, you'll be safe with me.'

'Thank you,' said Gráinne. 'Maisy is lovely, really lovely.'

'They all say she won't have much of a life because of her condition.'

'Stuff and Nonsense! Your little girl will outlive you and have a long life. She will give birth to a beautiful boy who will grow up and do great things. She will be happy. ***Believe*** what I say!'

Maisy's Mum looked at her, breathing very deeply.

'I believe you.'

'And now, before they both ask for bicycles, I think we should have a nice cup of nettle tea. I've been making a range of herbal teas to try out at the local markets. You can be my first customer.'

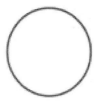

Let her be dedicated, consecrated, blood to blood, heart to heart, mind to mind, single in will, none without the circle, all to me

Book of Babalon

The village was agog at Maisy's miracle. The great and the good didn't believe the guff about antibiotics for one moment. As far as they were concerned, it was Mrs Figge's intense prayers that had done the trick and they were so glad she was part of their Bridge and Canasta clubs. She was suddenly far more interesting than her rather dreary husband. The great and the good even asked if she could give the odd sermon.

Miriam Figge was modest about it all, shy, self-deprecating - ever so appealing in her looking-at-the-floor and shuffling-her-feet way.

'Have you started wearing make-up?' asked Lady Bignall. 'It suits you. Brings out your panache, which we've all known you've always hidden.'

'And your trick-taking game has improved immeasurably,' added Mrs Champney-Warrener. 'I'd like to try some Double Dummy Bridge with you some time. Oh - and well done about that sad little mongol.'

Michael Figge didn't really know what to say. So he switched into the persona of Vicar and thanked Jesus and God and wrote a short piece in the *Winsley Weaver* without actually mentioned any names. He would do anything within his clerical power to stop his wife giving any kind of sermon. He wished he had someone to talk to about this, other than his bishop. Faith, he was beginning to realise, was never going to play Lady Chatterly to his Mellors.

Verily, in truth, he was inclined to think she was a *piqûre,* as they would say in France. A prick teaser. Plus, he had to admit, there was a social gap and intellectual gap between them that was becoming a chasm. Indeed, he had just stumbled upon an article by a fellow from his old Trinity College, Oxford, arguing that the word in the New Testament for carpenter – *tekton* – is more accurately translated as architect. And Michael Figge's own father was an architect! So Jesus was as middle class as he himself.

He wondered whether his own wife, whom he had inadvertently neglected over the years, might be worth courting again. She started to look rather attractive with the make-up she now wore, though he didn't ask why.

Publicly, Miriam Figge wore her shy, self-deprecating manner like her husband wore his gleaming dog-collar. Privately, she was becoming as big as Lilith had briefly been, and this would lead her into all sorts of highways and by-ways in future years that don't concern us here.

All the curiosity and love that she had shone toward Lily, blasting her like a big, waterproof, three-battery torch, was now turned onto herself and Maisy. Except she held the torch above them both, blasting down.

Maisy enjoyed this, although nothing and no-one would get between her and her best friend.

Maisy's Mum was aware of this happening but it did no-one any harm. Besides, Maisy would soon start at a 'special school' for what was then termed ESN(M) children. That is, Educationally Subnormal (Moderate). Despite the dreadful labels, the Magdalen Hospital School was a cheerful happy place. The council would pay for a taxi to take her down Winsley Hill, along the valley, then up Brassknocker Hill and into the village of Combe Down. It would take her ten minutes, and at the end of day she would be back playing with Lily again if she wanted.

During what Vicar Figge would call High Days and Holy Days, Granny and the Guardians did their own thing and during the Christmas period Lily went through all the public motions without actually engaging. She quite liked the idea of a cheery fellow riding in the sky among the stars and didn't try to spoil it for Maisy. Even so she was thrilled when, on Christmas Day, she came down and found a blue Realm Rider bicycle with red stabilisers, in front of the fireplace.

On that first Boxing Day, Granny and the Guardians did as they usually did: they opened up the village hall (quite separate from the church hall where Sunday School and Beetle Drives were held) and gave a free meal to the elderly (some of whom were ferried in by Hope and Chazza). The fact that it was free meant that the great and the good of Winsley Hill felt it was strictly for the lower classes and kept away.

The vicar was aware of these occasions and the closeness of the four women who didn't seem to mix outside of their clique.. They were affable to all but close to none. They almost always attracted more to their 'dos' and the free nosh and sing-along than he did offering the more important spiritual nourishment of the Words of the Lord.

Chazza paid for an outside caterers to bring the food and Granny unleashed a full range of her ciders and herbal teas but the truly memorable thing was, on that first Boxing Day (and other occasions afterwards), the elderly of the hill and valley were served their drinks by an unearthly, dark-eyed, dark haired little girl who barely peered over the top of the tables and whose gleaming bicycle was propped prominently in front of the stage.

Ooh she is so pretty!

Like a fairy!

I'd love another cuppa your tea, my lovely

And one a those cakes your granny makes.

Then Faith, Hope and Chazza got up on the stage and sang hits from the very first girl band in Britain in the 50s and 60s, called the Beverley Sisters. They sang golden oldies such as

Greensleeves, I Saw Mommy Kissing Santa Claus and even parodied some stuff by the Beatles.

Yeah Yeah Yeah chorused the room and Lily clapped, and even Lilith peered around from the far side and thought that there were worse places to be on Earth than this.

The oldies all felt better as the afternoon progressed:

Dulcie could now waggle her arthritic fingers.

Mabel had a significant lessening of her back pain.

Ted, who had seen great slaughter at Arnhem, found himself smiling again.

All around the room, of some two dozen folk, things were happening on many levels. None of it was dramatic. No-one leapt up crying out that -Hallelujah! - they had been cured. All of the improvements only just poked above the surface of their awareness, like the little girl's head poked above their tables. It was all spread by a nod and a wink, and a determination to enjoy the present and come to the next do.

'Have you put something in this?' asked Dennis, a veteran of Alamein in the North African Campaign, holding up his mug of tea.

'Bromide you mean?' said Chazza with a wink, who knew all about what the Army did during the war, and flirted outrageously with old soldiers.

'If I'd been thirty years younger,' Dennis sighed, giving her a leer.

'Or I'd been thirty years older!'

'Here, little Lily...get this old Desert Rat another tea would you? Extra strong!'

The only thing that Granny and the Guardians had to watch out for and deal with cleverly, were questions as to why Lily didn't eat. And that's because by this time Lily never ate. Or drank more than a few glasses of water or milk.. She knew enough to hide the fact in Sunday School but all the rest of the time her Big People covered up this fact as firmly as they covered her feet. Today, there seem to be a hundred thousand people across the world declaring themselves to be Lightarians – existing solely on sunlight or moonlight or even starlight. Most of them are self-deluded or outright frauds but a few have passed all the tests.

'Well she doesn't seem to suffer,' Faith had commented when they first noticed this.

'If it ain't broke, don't fix it,' advised Chazza.

On that first Boxing Day Lilith was equally occupied by glimpses of the little white-haired boy whom she had first met at the bottom of her garden.

Come in, she said with her mind, as his face pressed against the window of the kitchen, the saddest expression in his one blue eye and one green.

Can't he replied, then disappeared.

This happened several times and distracted her from the jollity. Granny and her aunts noticed the change in her tone and wondered – worried – if Lilith was going to do a Big One and astonish everyone and blow her cover.

And then the boy went – or rather Lilith became aware that he was no longer in the aura of her time and space, and she became Lily again, and joined in passing the parcels with its gifts of cheap perfume and strong cigarettes. And they finished off with Bingo and its top prize of £10 and she thought that the greatest game ever and made sure that the numbers came out right for the Desert Rat who didn't look anything like a rat.

'What a time,' whispered Dulcie as she left, flexing her fingers as if she might be about to coin tricks.

'Time is,' said the little girl, handing her the walking stick.

When the 1970s arrived Gráinne felt as though heavy lock gates had been opened at the end of a narrow canal, leading out into a broad and endless lake. For her and her sisters, it was a time of wonders: small wonders that actually had huge long-term impact; great wonders that they still needed to keep shtum about lest the sanctuary of the valley be disturbed.

There was the time when Maisy's Mum and Granny were chatting in the garden hanging out the washing, while their two little girls played indoors in Lilith's bedroom.

'What are you up to in there?' called Granny through the open window, smiling at their giggles.

'We're playing shoe shops!' said Lily.

'Maisy's favourite game! She'll have all your shoes out.'

Christ, swore Granny, dashing inside and up the stairs. If Maisy – or anyone – saw Lilith's bird-feet…

Maisy's Mum was right. Every shoe in the entire house, including the wellies that normally stayed in the downstairs porch, was on display in Lilith's room. And there was Maisy trying on her friend's special shoes and there was Lilith who paused when she saw Granny burst into the room and understood why.

'Look Granny,' she said, removing Maisy's shoes to show her bare feet and waggle her toes.

Christ, swore Granny again, who had no belief in the first such being. Lilith's feet were no longer bird-claws: now with four toes only, but human ones. She could even wear sandals in future and very few would notice.

Then there were several visits to the Chest Hospital with Hope, who just wanted the odd patient to be given a little boost and get discharged earlier. Little boosts were easy for Lilith to give, though when she was in full-on far-side mode she sometimes knew that not everybody can or even should be healed. Aunty Hope knew that better than anyone of course, and always deferred to her odd niece.

Lilith saw that one of the patients in particular, a young airman called Jonjo, was of particular interest to Hope. And he to her. If our Moonchild Lilith gained a sense of what human Guilt was like when she felt compelled to heal Maisy, she was hugely fascinated by this Love thing that was flashing back and forth between Hope and Jonjo. While the two big people strolled gently around the gardens holding hands with Lilith, she felt the current flowing. At every third step they lifted her off the ground and swung her over imaginary rivers and crocodile pits and Lily felt that they didn't have anything this much fun amid the Sirians.

They went to the thatched building that had a full-sized snooker table and Jonjo explained to Lilith how to play the game, and showed her how to stand on a chair and angle the cue so as not to rip the baize – which was apparently the biggest of crimes. She managed to pot a pink and a black but Aunty Hope, giggling in the background, was just hopeless when she tried, no matter how much Jonjo wrapped his arms around hers to guide her.

'Thank you Jonjo,' said Lilith when the game was over, and she did something that would lessen his cough for a little while.

'No, thank *you* for bringing your Aunty up here in the middle of nowhere to see a wreck like me. Please bring her again.'

'She will, oh she will!' smiled Hope, almost dancing.

Afterwards, they walked the back route down to Dicky Bird House, through the woods and past the caves where the bats lived, with the kind sign on the rocks that you can still see, saying:

TRESPASSERS BEWARE OF FALLING STONES
Hope sighed.

'Don't worry Lilith. I know you can't do a Maisy on him.'

'Sorry Aunty.'

'Don't be sorry you daft little thing! But he's beautiful isn't he? So gentle and wise. I want to be with him forever. And now that I know *you'll* be safe...'

The last time anyone saw Hope alive was when she drove up to the sanatorium from Dicky Bird House in her Renault 4. A very jolly woman dressed all in black waved to them all from the passenger seat. Hope leaned over and joined in. It looked like they were going to a party.

'Is that Aunty Hope's mum?'

'No, that's the full-time Angel of Death. She will take Jonjo and Hope to a happy place together.'

'Tonight,' said Faith, 'if you look up toward the Pleiades you'll only be able to see six.'

Lilith did more than that, she went up there at night and didn't care who saw her zooming, and saw Hope-as-Was toward the back of the cluster, out of sight, but with a softer radiance this time, caused by being joined as One with Jonjo-as-Was, so it was hard to tell where one ended and the other began.

We've never been so happy, they burbled when Lilith returned.

And then there was the time when Chazza took Lilith into the City of Bath to get her some *proper* shoes, and fitted for the uniform needed to start Junior School. She was growing up nicely. It all went well until they passed a newsagents on Pulteney Bridge with copies of *The Sun* screaming out that Slicky Vicky had been jailed for peddling drugs.

Lilith was cold and far removed from any torment; Lily was still little-girl enough to feel upset about this happening to the best Mummy in the World

Chazza hugged her, wouldn't buy the newspaper and walked on.

'She'll be okay Lil.'

'No she won't.'

Chazza knew not to reason with or fight prescience.

'Come on lets go down to the river and see the swans.'

Pulteney Weir was – and is – a great crescent of foaming, churning white water that joins the two halves of the tiny city together. The negative ions always created a carnival atmosphere between the worlds and when the river was in flood it was often hard to hear yourself talk. Strings of colourful narrowboats and other small craft were moored along the length of the river creating its own alternative community.

'When I am a big girl, I will get one like that,' said Lily, who loved a boat she saw called Kelby, with its smoking chimney, bags of coal on the stern deck, bicycles stored upside down on the roof, rectangular window frames with rounded corners, hanging baskets, a coir doormat and a glimpse inside of bedroom, lounge and kitchen. She loved Dicky Bird House, but the thought of a cosy home on a river also had attractions. In fact the boat was as magical as anything she could have found across the galaxy.

'When you're grown up Lil, you will get whatever you want.'

A young man and woman inside waved out to her. They would have invited her into their floating home bobbing on the grey river but she sensed a turbulence of a very different kind coming on the tow-path behind.

A man was looking at her. His face was grey and frightened. If he'd been a leaf you could say he was shaking from top to bottom.

Aunty Chaz didn't know who he was or if he was having some sort of a stroke.

Lilith, who never forgot names, said:

'Hello. Dr McHaffee.'

McHaffee himself could never have explained his reaction. For a moment, when he saw that little girl completely out of context, he had the sense of being back in Kenneth Grant's room, being influenced on subtle levels by all manner of dirty, joyless, alien consciousness. He was aware that he must have looked like a complete lunatic standing there shaking his arms, but the girl induced instant, cold and illogical terror within him. All he could think about was her feet – the bird feet of the Night Demon. Here it was now, before him, bringing out all his guilts.

Chazza, who had had commando-level training during the War, pulled Lilith behind her. She had blown up, stabbed or simply shot a few Obersturmbannführers in her time. Whoever this wretch was, she didn't want him simply to walk away and cause mayhem later. There was no-one else around, she could do this quickly.

'Come here you little shit,' she whispered. Then: 'Sorry about the language, Lil.'

In the event she didn't have to do a thing. A flight of swans dived onto him, knocking him over. For a moment you couldn't see anything but flapping, cracking wings and hear the swans snorting and hissing.

Stop now, said Lilith to them and they did, and they backed off as a bloodied McHaffee ran off across the rugby field.

'Who was that, Lil?'

'A friend. That's what he once told me.'

The swans, silent now, flowed around Lilith like snow.

In all the excitement, Chazza had dropped the bags she was carrying containing two boxes of Lily's gleaming new shoes, which scattered over the tow-path. She was about to scoop them up when another fellow appeared and beat her to it.

'Oh!' she said, because for a moment it looked like the comedian Billy Connolly, although she soon saw it wasn't. This fella was a dirtier version, and probably a rough sleeper by the look of his clothes. He must have witnessed everything.

'Here, lassy,' he said, taking one of the shoes and bowing before the little girl, offering to fit it. 'Ye *shall* go tae the ball!'

Lilith laughed. She didn't often laugh. The man gleamed. An otherness flowed between them that was obvious to Chazza. As one of the intra-class, she sensed all kinds of odd beings that sneaked into the outerworld – especially on the streets of Bath.

'Who are you, sir?'

The man put the new shoes neatly back into their boxes and safely into the carrier bags, handing them back with a bow.

'The Right Reverend Robert Kirk, late of Aberfoyle, at yurr service, young ladies.'

Chazza was disappointed. She rather hoped it *would* be the rude and rumbustious Billy Connolly.

149

'I see...you're one of those time travellers. Seem to be a lot of you around lately. Well, travel on, cheerie-oh, things to do!'

Kirk gave a deep bow. Lilith touched his brow at the lowest point. He gasped, then sighed. Whatever things within his soul that had been broken now seemed to be fixed. He straightened, looked down at the little girl.

'I am perplexed, lassie. You are nocht the Giftie, are ye?'

Lilith shook her head.

'You will find her.'

'Where? Oh where?'

'Follow Dr McHaffee...'

The Right Reverend Robert Kirk looked across the field to the disappearing figure and made after him.

Chazza didn't follow any of this. Then again, when Lilith was full-on, all she could do was step aside and realise that there were Mysteries being worked that even she as one of the intra-class would never fully grasp.

'Come on, Lily, come and see my charity clothes shop. You can serve the customers.'

'Can I have a narrowboat?'

'Should we worry about this McHaffee?' asked Chazza of Gráinne when they met again.

'I don't think so. I don't feel there is any real link. Apparently he's opened a private care home in Bath for troubled souls called House of Dreams, or some such. I never met him, but my Vicky rather ran rings around him, apparently, and got him sacked from the hospital. And he wrote one rather useless book called 'Autism – Entering the Silence' which seems to have been based upon his attempts to understand Lilith in the Children's Home. The cheek!'

'Let me know if you need me to sort him.

'I really don't think we need worry about him,' she decreed, using her own formidable clairvoyance and trusting it, even though on many occasions it could be wrong.

Years went by that seemed like days. Lilith made the normal transition from teeny-tiny girl to quite big girl without anyone really noticing. There were storms, riots, wars, national strikes and political chaos in Britain and across the world while above them - 62 miles above - men in space suits were trying to conquer the Moon. The Apollo programmes, still using the rocket fuel pioneered by Jack Parsons, saw another five missions landing men on the Moon, ending with Apollo 17 that spent three days there.

Then the Americans and Russians got together in low earth orbit above Granny's head to join together a Soyuz spacecraft with an American Command Module. They created some kind of entente in space where they couldn't quite on Earth.

And all the while the Americans worked furiously on the Space Shuttle which would fly above the valley and hill also.

Lilith, growing slowly and thus imperceptibly closer to the Moon, watched it all. The astronauts were never quite alone. Sometimes what they thought were UFO's flashing past were nothing more than the lights of a glittering little girl whose body 62 miles below was in training to be the Messiah, or next Christ, or World Saviour - name Her how you will.

Granny was not impressed by this distance when Lilith quoted it:

'Stuff and You-Know-What! I drive further than that every day to some of my markets!'

But for Gráinne there were tumults of her own to deal with. Her daughter Vicky refused all attempts to engage. If it wasn't for the tabloids, Gráinne would never what she was up to. What she did learn was never good. Sometimes she wondered if Vicky had ever said: *My mum is the best mum in the world.* She doubted it. If she herself had been a Moonchild wannabe, she was never able to balance the human with the supra-human, as Lilith clearly could. Vicky herself, whom Lilith so strongly resembled, had been a little star until the drugs.

Once, when Lilith was curled in her lap and watching *The Railway Children*, she asked:

'Granny… what about Grandad? Where is he?'

Big long pause from Granny.

'You know Lilith, I don't know where he is, or even who he is. Some people might still think that terrible in this day and age but I know you won't.'

'I don't.'

'I was at a shindig arranged by Warminster Barracks. This was just after the War when us Land Army girls were being disbanded and numbers of soldiers de-mobbed, as they called it. You can imagine it was a bit wild, we were all so happy it had ended. That's when I first got my taste for cider. I danced with any number of soldiers but I don't think anything happened. I was a good dancer. I preferred dancing to anything. I wasn't always big and clumpy like now! One of them chatted me up. Well he didn't need to.

'So your grandfather was a sergeant in the British Army. Or that's what he seemed. I knew – and he knew that I knew – that he came from a faraway world behind the Sun. There was a lot of light that night. And that's all you need to know. And remember what it's not about?'

'Not about spaceships.'

'No. Well, I don't think so. Maybe it was. Maybe it is. You'll find out yourself some day. So to finish answering: *I* was born in 1922 in the middle of the Irish Civil War that everyone in this country has forgotten now. I don't know the details but the local priest tried to exorcise my mother while she giving birth! Or so I was told. Apparently he tried to throw me on the fire but… *people*… came and saved me. So mum fled to England but died shortly after and my dad remarried. I never got to learn the truth of my birth, or who the *people* were and to be honest I don't want to go inward and spy. I just live in the present.'

Don't be sad said Lilith to her mind when she saw Granny brooding. *You always get sad after you do the washing.*

Sorry

152

*Don't be sorry, you daft big thing. **My** mummy won't be with us much longer.*

Nor was she. When they saw the news on the BBC of her death by overdose, neither of them was surprised or even saddened.

Meteors burn up, they both thought.

The valley acted for Granny like one of the trenches in the Great War: The man-made demons of social and international hate seemed to shoot above Dicky Bird House and explode elsewhere, keeping them safe from any shrapnel. All she needed was to tend her garden, and make sure that Lily continued to fit in at school while hiding her true self.

At least she could remove her shoes for Physical Exercise and swimming and dance lessons now!

In fact this new-fangled term 'autism' created a perfect disguise and McHaffee's book offered all sorts of options. She showed it to all her teachers at both the junior and later her secondary school and bulleted the crucial points:

- Delayed speech development or not speaking at all
- Frequent repetition of set words and phrases
- Speech that sounds very monotonous or flat
- Preferring to communicate using single words, despite being able to speak in sentences

And then there was:

- No interest in interacting with other people, including children of a similar age
- Not enjoying situations that most children of their age like, such as birthday parties
- Preferring to play alone
- Rarely using gestures or facial expressions when communicating

But she did think once to herself: *Oh my goodness, this is Lilith to a T. Maybe McHaffee's book is actually right? Maybe the Moonchild is necessarily autistic. And maybe all autistic people are Moonchildren?!*

So Lilith was left alone although, given her extraordinary inner life, she was never lonely. The other children still wanted to be her friend and get invited down to meet the goat and her tame owl and friendly snake and were somewhat jealous of Maisy who had access to all these.

It was the same when she started secondary school and – in the years when children would actually walk – she did so by herself every day. A leisurely stroll of 40 minutes if she took the top road over the hill, during which she engaged with all sorts of inner beings in the fields at either side of the road to Bradford on Avon. Or somewhat longer if she took 'the pretty way' along the river and parallel canal at the bottom of the valley.

Maisy still came to spend quality time with her first and best friend before the Lilith left school and the valley. Even though the latter was no longer able to become teeny-tiny Lily again completely, she rather liked being able to come down a few levels and be child-like again.

Her experience there at Fitzmaurice School mirrored that of her quietly blissful time at St Barbara's. Lilith stopped any jealousy. She also stopped any bullying. It was not that she needed to say anything or utter any reproach. Quietly, without anyone realising, she seemed to reach into deep places that brought out the best. Usually she did no more than touch a shoulder and say *Time Is*, under her breath, and it worked from there.

The big girls and bigger boys all accepted that Lilith was different. They didn't try to punish her for it. They all grew in differing ways, and levels. Numbers of them created the fad of sponsored walks or swims for local charities. Not one of them suffered from acne or period pains. Ba Ba Babalon indeed...

Things came to a head before her 13th birthday when she was snatched, at a time when the full moon was out and like a skull, and the fields across the valley were stiff with golden wheat.

It was because of the butterfly net again. Although it still stood where it had been planted at her first arrival, the net itself had been sealed at its opening to make sure that no butterfly would ever be trapped within its tube. It just acted as a grey windsock that would show Granny whether it was good drying weather outside.

Lilith noticed that, somehow, a little bat had got inside and was struggling.

Be still, she said. *I will get you out.*

So she did. As there was still daylight she could hardly release it here. Much as she was friends with Owl she knew that Bat would be seen as a perfect snack. Besides she just loved the feel of its tiny body and wings and the eyes that were so much like her own.

I will take you home...

Although she had passed the caves many times before when foraging in the woods with Granny she had never been there alone. Despite regular warnings never to wander off, there was only so much caution that a true Moonchild could take. And the baby bat in her warm hands was excited and telling her all sorts of things. It was like having a sister.

The caves were covered with metal grills that would allow the clever bats full access but stop any moronic humans getting in. She put her hand through and released her little sister, and could sense at the far end of the cave the collective consciousness of the whole colony.

I have got wings like yours she told them, rather smugly, and from the darkness of the old mine came a rush of greeting and all sorts of ancient pictures from a Time before Time. She was thrilled. If people today talk casually about having totem animals then Lilith's were always going to be Bat and Owl.

She could have stood there all day listening to and being part of the great silent song they were making inside. She was so enrapt that she never heard the man sneaking up behind to put a hood over her head, grab her and carry her off like a carpet so that her legs were raked by the branches of the trees and she lost one of her shoes.

While Hope may have 'gone on', as some say, she hadn't abandoned her duties as a Guardian. Now, if you can use such a temporal term for a timeless state, she was still watching over the Moonchild from other levels.

Go to Lilith! she told Faith, Chazza and Granny. *Go to the woods*....

They heard. They dropped everything.

Faith took her hammer. In the days before women bought whistles, rape alarms and pepper sprays for their personal protection Faith had always found that a sharp blow from a simple hammer would stop anyone.

Chazza, who had no need for personal protection, took her knuckleduster and the commando dagger that she honed and polished on a weekly basis.

Gráinne fired up within herself all the awesome and terrifying powers of the Granny who would use any level of violence up to and including death in order to protect her brood.

In the end, it was almost comical...

The got to the woods just as dusk was beginning to flow. In the natural lay-by that was opposite the caves they saw a small van that might once have had a different colour but was now completely black: the windscreen, windows, bonnet, lights, wheel arches, entire bodywork. At first Faith thought it belonged some idiot who had covered his whole vehicle in fur – there were a lot of people doing wacky things with cars in that year. But as they came nearer, running, looking everywhere and listening inwardly for clues as to Lilith's whereabouts, it was Granny who twigged.

'Bats,' she gasped, somewhat breathless. 'And I'm sure that's Zak's van.'

Inside, beneath the living pelt, they could hear someone trying to start the engine which was giving no more than wheezy coughs. They could hear Lilith's voice in their heads telling the bats to go, and thanking them. The bats peeled away at once like black smoke and spiralled off to their nearby roosts.

When they yanked open the door and saw her tied up on the back seat with the hood still covering her head, it was only her command *Do not hurt him* that stopped Chazza slicing his throat.

Zak sat behind the wheel, terrified. As much by Lilith's calm indifference to her plight, as by her ability to summon the bats and stop his engine.

'Gráinne,' he started, 'I know what you must be thinking, but….'

He didn't finish. Gráinne leaned in and slapped him several times despite what Lilith had said. Chazza did the same from the other side. He made no resistance. Faith got in behind and removed the hood as Chazza sliced the tapes binding Lilith's arms.

Lilith smiled. She was having an adventure.

Granny showed all the strength she had gained from years of labouring on the land and dragged her erstwhile boyfriend out by his long, greying hair.

'Zak you rotten bastard. We are now going to have a *serious* talk.'

Thank you, she then said to the dancing spirit of Hope, who was now thoroughly enjoying the events. *Off you go back to our stars...*

Of course, it was a full moon now, in a clear sky. They dragged Zak to the place in the garden beyond the apple trees

157

where Time is not quite what it should be. In the kind of No Mans Land between Granny's garden and the Manor was a large, old ruinous stable that hadn't been used for years. Perhaps there should have been a manger but instead they had a tree growing into the side. Moonlight poured through the hole in the roof. The women used that as a searchlight on his face as they pushed Zak into an old rusty garden chair. Chazza used the tape she had found in his car to bind his arms.

Granny, said Lilith, turning away from the curious Owl who had perched there to watch. *I do not want you to hurt him.*

He tried to hurt you.

He will not do that again.

She seemed indifferent to the events. A whole family of badgers made their way through a break in the back wall of the stable; she wanted a good chat with the cubs.

Zak was terrified. He had soiled himself.

'*Theeey* will come for me, he sobbed, emphasising that word as Lilith's mum had once pronounced *Mooon*child

'Stuff and nonsense.'

'Who are *They*, exactly?' asked Faith.

'What are *They* exactly?' came Chazza.

'Stuff and nonsense and ninety-three doses of taradiddle! Heard it all before.'

And so she had. She knew that every being on every planet has fears of *Them*, and how *They* might bring terror, torment and despair. But *They* are not so much monsters that the First Lilith was said to inspire, but can be: tax inspectors, bad neighbours, in-laws, creditors, bank managers, lawyers – the list is infinite. In the eyes of the Rothschilds (whom some say are the secret rulers of this world), *They* are the great unwashed who might one day rise up; in the eyes of lonely boys who wake at night in a cold sweat dreading the morning, *They* are the school bullies. Even the Reptoids from the Draco star system see the Sirians as *Them.*

They are simply our greatest dreads: the very shapes of our fears made manifest before our brows. Granny, who had lived her life as something of an atheist mystic or mystical atheist, had no time for the sort of quivering that Zak was doing now. Bring *Them* on, as far as she was concerned.

'You've known about us all along haven't you Zak?'

'No.'

'I thought you were just after my runner beans.'

'No. I was recruited. By some colonel. Formed a new department for national security. DI15. Defence Intelligence 15. Already told you too much.'

'Name?'

'Dunno. Honest.'

Chazza stopped throwing her dagger into the side wall of the stable.

'A colonel? Describe him.'

'Sort of burnt face on one side. Brushed his hair to cover it. Please let me go. I'm afraid *It* will come.'

Granny had even less time for the *Its* of this world than she had for *Them.* But Chazza's eyes widened.

'That's Waggo! My old mate Colonel Waghorn! Or I *thought* he was a mate. The bastard...'

'We saw you on your silly chair, Zak. In Porton Down.'

'It's not silly. It plugs into my brain. It enables things.'

'We can plug into your brain without any stupid wires.'

'Don't. I don't want *It* to come. *It* came once and escaped. Then it came back into me and gave me nightmares. *It* made me try and grab the girl.'

'Taraddidle,' said Granny, although she didn't doubt him. Her great-granny really did extrude ectoplasm and it was never cheese-cloth, no matter what the doubters sneered, and the figures she manifested were – it was said – extraordinary.

'Make it come now, Zak. We want to see it.'

'I'm not plugged into anything. I haven't taken the stuff they gave me. I don't want to see it! Please, I don't want to see it!'

'Why do people always say *please* when they're about to get a knife stuck into them?' asked Chazza, who understood that she was under strict instructions from Lilith not to hurt the man.

'*We* will plug into you. Shut up.'

He had no choice. When you've got three women with smidgens of Anunnaki blood (and god knows what else) within them, surrounding you and shoving their astral fingers into your brain like psychic surgeons, then it really is best to just shut up.

'Lie back and think of Sumer,' teased Faith.

And when Lilith herself stopped talking to the badgers and stood before him there was a whirlwind in his raddled psyche. In the white fire of the moonlight, in a zone in the garden where Time sort of pauses amid broken and shadowy things, they did things within his brain and mind.

He looked as if he might have screamed but Lilith touched his lips and he didn't. 'Nine Moons,' was all she said, although even the Guardians never fathomed that one exactly. It started like a sort of silvery, astrally bubbling out of his body, all up and down his front, as if each of the chakras was determined to get involved in this. The bubbles grew and shrank, then grew bigger and shrank less. The whole of Zak's front was soon covered in the translucence, reflecting light, reflecting faces, pushing out from his body in an obscene act of birth.

Lilith stood before him unmoved, detached, expressionless. The three women standing behind him, hands on his head and astral fingers into his brain, were transfixed. They had never seen *this* before!

The blob separated from Zak completely except for a thin umbilical into his gut. It started to take shape. This was the moment of his greatest terror when he had to face the Thing all over again. First the hint of legs, though not quite touching the ground; then the trunk and a stubby suggestion of arms; and finally the small blob of an obscenely featureless head.

'Hello,' said Lilith in the calmest of voices, which seemed to empower the creature into taking a more perfect shape.

'Hello, Lilith,' it replied in the clearest of tones as it hardened into the shape of a naked little white-haired boy with different coloured eyes. It seemed to become aware of its nakedness and instantly fashioned modern clothes.

The umbilical connecting him with Zak dissolved. The three women looked on with astonishment. Zak fainted and they just left him slumped in the chair. The stable was filled with a kind of amniotic light, if you can imagine such a thing.

'Tell me your name,' said Lilith, but there was a taunting tone as if she already knew.

'Adam. You already know that.'

'We've been apart a long time.'

'Silly things have been done.'

'We were once together.'

'We can be again.'

Come here, she said in her mind although everyone could hear and even the owl in the rafters gave a hoot of excitement.

So he did, and she seemed to absorb him into her own body as if he was no more than mist, and when it was complete she whispered *At the last* and hugged herself and danced on the spot and muttered all sorts of things in an ancient tongue that meant nothing to the watchers.

'What just happened?' asked Granny out loud.

'Buggered if I know,' answered Chazza. 'Something to do with Genesis I suppose. She's a least an inch taller and a few pounds heavier!'

Really, they would have had to look into the oldest mirror, back to the oldest times in the furthest, darkest reaches of Lilith's Cave to get any real understanding of that moment.

'Just look at her! *Look!*' exclaimed Faith.

They all did, and if at times in the past she had seemed like a bomb about to explode, *this* little girl was a fusion machine. If you could have plugged her into the National Grid she could have given free energy to every house along the Wiltshire and Somerset border. She held up her hands as if in surrender. There seemed to be a little heart scarred on each palm.

'Don't worry Granny and Aunties,' she soothed, though in a slightly lower voice than before – no longer a little girl's tones. 'But we're tired now and want to go to bed...'

'Is that a royal 'we'?' whispered Chazza following on behind after they released the spent Zak and went back to Dicky Bird House.

'I think there's two of them now,' mused Faith.

At one point, on the rough path, Lilith stumbled but Granny caught her and carried her the rest of the way. Then up the stairs and into bed, with the teddy next to her. She seemed luminous. The room shone for the rest of the night.

'She's still our little girl.'

'She's more than that now, Granny...'

The guardian women were not really individuals as we might understand the term. Of course they had Free Will and much of the human stuff, but there was an element of the hive about them: they gravitated toward each other without needing to make any contact that we might see.

So one night, in mid-winter, just as it was beginning to snow, they all found themselves down at the cottage. The fire was roaring, the telly was off, they drank hot chocolate in big mugs and knew that Lilith was upstairs asleep. They gossiped and reminisced but there was an underlying thrill about them like children awaiting Santa.

Outside, through the curtains, there was a great light.

Nammu is here they all thought, and when someone knocked on the front door in the most human of ways the three of them sprinted to answer it, although Granny got there first muttering about it being *her* house so she should be first.

Outside, in the snow, in her nurses' uniform, was Sister Ndlovu.

Nammu, they said in some awe, for they knew that this was an echo of the Being who, in a land far from their valley, a million years before, was believed to have given birth to the earth and heavens and all the later Anunnaki.

But you can call me Mary! Mary Endlove. Nammu's just a title like Granny and Aunty. I've got a sort of a taxi waiting for me so I can't stay long. Where is my Lilith?

Lilith stood behind them, slightly distressed.

We can't sleep she said. *Me and the Adam. Hello Nammu...*

Sister Ndlovu, for we might as well call her that in this form, gave a huge smile.

Oh my... Look how you've grown! Are you too big to be cuddled now?

No.

Sister Ndlovu took the big chair in front of the fire and Lilith curled into her lap as she had done in the Children's Home and sighed.

'Things to say, things to tell,' Sister said out loud, with her deep voice like the sea. 'It begins now, you all know that. Granny will have told you some of it. Now hear it from me, the Source. Are you sitting comfortably?' she asked with a chuckle, paying homage to the *Listen with Mother* story-times that had had Lily glued to the telly when growing up.

They all nodded. They were all wide-eyed and in awe. They were all children.

'You, my little Lilith, my daughter, are pure Anunnaki. It took us a long time to make you happen. But Granny, you have to think of the Anunnaki now – the real ones – as more like viruses, working through the bloodstream.

'We made so many mistakes when we first came to Earth. My two sons did bad things, but I blame myself. They told me that I was the best mum in Nibiru. I was so flattered that I let them run amok. Enki had all the intellect in the universe but no simple intelligence and he created The Adam to do all his work. Then he ordered you, Lilith, to become The Adam's first wife. En-Lil resented all this. He never had much personality - and much of *that* was bad. He let people turn him into the dreadful Jehovah and then messed up the whole world. But you met an echo of him once didn't you? You met a boy with the teeniest tiniest bit of En-Lil the Anunnaki in him, remember?'

'Wayne. He broke my butterfly net.'

'And what did you do to him?'

'I cured his spots. I was kind. He fixed the net.'

'And he is now the kindest boy you could meet. So this is how it will work from now. The highest principles of the Anunnaki will be passed on like viruses working through the bloodstreams of the soul. By simple, silent touch. It will be like playing tag – you and Maisy play tag don't you?'

'Will there be spaceships?' asked Granny, frowning.

'I thought you'd ask that!' she laughed. 'Personally, if you want to see me in some sort of Mothership coming down to whisper good news, then I won't object. Some people need that.'

'She's the Messiah, isn't she?' asked Faith.

'Or the Christ?'

'Oh I do NOT like those terms! Lilith, the Lady Babalon, our Moonchild, will never be more than a blue-lidded daughter of the Moon. There will be no sacred Holy Books that people can mistranslate or expand upon years afterwards or use as weapons.

'There will be no people being burnt, tortured, abused, beheaded, scorned, rejected or punished because they believe or do not believe.

'There will be no special garments, rituals, ceremonies, celebrations or publicity in any shape or form.

'There will be no clamour or brutal attempts to overthrow existing religions.

'There will be no followers or missionaries or priests or priestesses. There will be no sacrifice, crucifixions, talks of redeemers or original sin – although quiet, personal attempts at atonement will be acceptable for wrongs done by an individual.

'Adam wronged Lilith in the earliest of tales when he dumped her and ran off with Eve. But that is all made good now, isn't it?'

Lilith nodded. 'We're happy,' she whispered, hugging herself.

'And that, my dearest ladies, is that! I suppose, in modern terms, she *is* the Christ, but through the slow spread of loving-kindness the people will *all* absorb her new virus in time. They will *all* become a new form of Christ yet never talk about it, and pass it on through this game of tag that Lilith is starting. They will *all* be Messiahs in their private lives. This is the way new worlds begin: not with a bang but a whisper.'

There was silence in the room. Granny put more logs on the fire. The fire crackled and threw their shadows on the walls: in the small glowing caves between its burning logs they all had images of other Beginnings, even long before Sumer. Outside, Owl was heard hooting in the snow.

After a long moment Granny shifted in her seat and offered: 'Would you like some hot chocolate?'

Sister Ndlovu laughed. Lilith sat up in her lap and kissed her on the cheek.

'Oh my lovely, as they say hereabouts… I will always be watching out for you my little Moonchild. But now, I think I heard my taxi outside.'

They stood aside as she went to the door. Cold blasted in. The snow was deep by this time and the night silent. Lilith called out an awkward goodbye from behind them which made them look back into the house; when they turned again to wave to Sister Ndlovu there was only the utterly mute, empty snow-clad garden. Her footprints in the snow simply stopped as if she had been lifted into the dark sky.

'Maybe it *is* about spaceships!' muttered Granny.

What happened to the rest after Nammu's visit and the start of Lilith's mission?

Granny Gráinne stayed within Dicky Bird House and may well be there yet, for all anyone knows. Like Lilith, like Snake, she is seen when she wants to be, although she must be very very old now as judged by human terms.

Chazza was outraged by Colonel Waghorn's perfidy. Her last known defence of Lilith came after exclaiming: 'I saved Waghorn's rotten life twice. Leave him to me. I'll put a stop to that End of the Pier show of his.' And she did. In the unwritten, unknowable and unseen histories of the Security Services she did just that.

Once Lilith started secondary school and Faith no longer needed to keep an eye on Vicar Figge, she left his employ and turned up on the doorstep of a certain Harold Stagge, in Limpley Stoke. Here, she used all her arts to learn all of *his* secrets but did her best to leave him – and the valley - in a better state than before. She really did break his heart in a way that was told long before that episode Lilith had seen in *Sooty and Sweep*. Yet she also put it back together in a much better way so that the Merlin of Limpley Stoke no longer cried lonely tears in the night.

Zak, after being touched on both brows by Lilith-plus on that epic night in the stable, disappeared into the glazed heart of Glastonbury, imagining it was Avalon. He never spoke a word of his encounter to anyone. In fact he could never quite remember what had happened, but would often break into sweat if he saw – or even thought about - white-haired little boys.

Vicar Figge's wife divorced him and he gave up the ministry. After many false starts he began to teach first aid skills for St John's Ambulance, where he found that saving bodies was better than saving souls. Years later when he eventually lost his *snobbisme* he had rather a pleasant relationship with Maisy's Mum.

It was the investigative journalist Maxy Mack who continued on the trail of Lilith long after she had disappeared from everyone else's minds. In fact it was he who had created the name 'Slicky Vicky' for her mother in the first place and had pursued her – and exposed her – in the tabloids with the sort of obsession that would get him jailed or heavily sued today. Some would call it love.

After Vicky's death he devoted himself to trying to find the deformed child that a few of the junkies in her circle babbled about – none of them coherently. *Just say Ba-Ba-Babalon and she'll come*, was the best he could get from them. He actually tried that once, but started having dreams of a blue-lidded woman who taunted him, so he stopped that. In the 70s there were an awful lot of Homes for children like her. He started doorstepping but drew a blank at them all. In fact at one in north London he felt positively threatened with violence. Not being a brave man and having a teeny-tiny shred of guilt about his quest for such a broken mite, he gave up on that quest. His attempts to find the girl's father were even less successful, and he was actually visited by Men in Black who made it quite clear that he was in danger of death if he persisted.

He came to believe, instead, that Vicky had been part of a cabal that included high and mighty people with odd connections: the very dubious MP and traitor Tom Driberg, for example, who had been involved in the (then illegal) gay scene with the gangster Ronnie Kray - and before that with the notorious Aleister Crowley. At one point he fancied that Slicky Vicky had faked her death and was carrying on with her mission as the mysterious Lady Babalon. And so he got it into his head (or was it planted by Gráinne?) that a female Dark Adept was influencing what *he* defined as the Ruling Families of the world, including the Rothschilds, Kennedys, Sinclairs and Windsors. He actually gravitated near to Lilith on many occasions without knowing; he never quite twigged that it was a little child who was the final piece in the jigsaw.

It wasn't that she had – or has – any powers of invisibility. The skills she needed to stay hidden – to stay 'occult' - she learned from Snake, who taught her how to slither and slide between events, shedding her skin when needed and finding safe and unexpected places to hide. The nearest that Maxy Mack ever came to Lilith was, in a sense, in the remnants of that skin she cast off, which soon decayed into the earth.

Yet he created a modern myth as to where this Dark Adept whom some called Lady Babalon might be found, and over the years the urban myth-makers joined in.

Lady Babalon was: a teacher in Eton, influencing future Prime Minsters; an employee in McDonald's in Belfast, spreading peace among her customers; a scientist in Porton Down making it more ethical, or in Rudloe Manor speaking to the aliens; a scientist in NASA preparing for Disclosure about what had *really* been going on above our heads; a cleaner in Downing Street; a fruit and veg seller in the Brick Lane market in London; a super mathematician working on String Theories and Hyperspace; a bicycle-repair woman living on a barge in the Kennet and Avon Canal; a transgender social worker in an adoption agency. The list is ever-becoming and near endless, depending on human need and hope.

And what about us, reading this, who now have the image of the Lady Babalon in our psyches?

At some point in the next few hours you will look at the palm of your hand to see if there is a slight blemish that might be considered heart-shaped. If there is not, you will still think of the best and highest kindness that you might want to pass onto to someone else without them knowing. Then you will decide that tomorrow you will touch them gently and discreetly, whispering *Time Is*, while visualising the best possible outcome for them – possibly in *Nine Moons*. You may not heal wounds or raise things from the dead, but you can be a ripple in the wave of Time and all its energies.

You might even help this long this by drawing a small heart on one palm and take it from there, without telling a soul.

At some point in the future – and this will happen – you will be startled when someone does this to you. And if you want to whisper *Ba-Ba-Babalon* and raise a private toast to Jack Parsons when next you look at the rising Moon making long shadows on the grass, then that's your own Mystery in place and your own far side waiting to be explored...

The Book of Babalon

The *Book of Babalon*, more accurately known as *Liber 49*, was channelled by Jack Parsons between January 4 and March 4, 1946. He saw himself as Belarion, the Antichrist, who had come to strip away all the nonsense and corruption and injustice of the Christian Era.

Parsons believed that this was the completion of *Liber Al vel Legis,* in effect the fourth and final book of the trilogy which had been received by Aleister Crowley in 1904, from an entity called Aiwass.

Do I personally accept the Book of Babalon as a continuation of Crowley's odd, disturbing and highly influential *Book of the Law?*

No, not at all. I don't doubt that 'in there' is a rather attractive and powerful energy that might respond to the name Lady Babalon. As she described herself to Belarion: 'I am the blue-lidded daughter of sunset, I am the naked brilliance of the voluptuous night sky.'

What's not to like about Her? But I go along with Granny Gráinne's idea that *Liber 49* was a good try, with some real gems within it, and that if Parson had been able to get his own tumultuous love life stable, then this personal Holy Book might have less staccato rhythms. Some of the statements, I feel, are actually personal cries for help, but you must judge for yourself.

The entire text of the *Book of Babalon* is available at various sites on-line. I print here the 77 'utterances' to look at.

Make of the following what you will. But do remember that Jack Parsons invoked the Lady Babalon to see the end of, in his words: servile virtues and superstitious restrictions; slave morality, prudery and shame; guilt and sin and the end to all authority that is not based on courage and manhood; the authority of lying priests, conniving judges, blackmailing police; the end to servile flattery and the coronations of mediocrities and the ascension of dolts.

What's not to like about that agenda under the influence of Lady Babalon?

He might have failed in almost all of that, but never forget that he helped get us to the Moon, and that his magick was as much a fuel in achieving that as the stuff which was used in the rockets...

LIBER 49

1. Yea, it is I, BABALON.

2. And this is my book, that is the fourth chapter of the Book of the Law, He completing the Name, for I am out of NUIT by HORUS, the incestuous sister of RA-HOOR-KHUIT.

3. It is BABALON. TIME IS. Ye fools.

4. Thou hast called me, oh accursed and beloved fool.

5-8. (Missing and presumed lost.)

9. Now know that I, BABALON, would take flesh and come among men.

10. I will come as a penelous (sic) flame, as a devious song, a trumpet in judgement halls, a banner before armies.

11. And gather my children unto me, for THE TIME is at hand.

12. And this is the way of my incarnation. Heed!

13. Thou shalt offer all thou art and all thou hast at my altar, witholding nothing. And thou shalt be smitten full sore and thereafter thou shalt be outcast and accursed, a lonely wanderer in abominable places.

14. Ye Dare. I have asked of none other, nor have they asked. Else is vain. But thou hast willed it.

15. Know then that thus I came to thee before, thou a great Lord, and I a maid enrapt. Ah blind folly.

16. And thereafter madness, all in vain. Thus it has been, multi- form. How thou hast burned beyond.

17. I shall come again, in the form thou knowest. Now it shall be thy blood.

18. The altar is aright, and the robe.

19. The perfume is sandal, and the cloth green and gold. There is my cup, our book, and thy dagger.

20. There is a flame.

21. The sigil of devotion. Be it consecrated, be it true, be it daily affirmed. I am not scorned. Thy love is to me. Procure a disk of copper, in diameter three inches paint thereon the field blue the star gold of me, BABALON.

22. It shall be my talisman. Consecrate with the supreme rituals of the word and the cup.

23. My calls as thou knowest. All love songs are of me. Also seek me in the Seventh Aire.

24. This for a time appointed. Seek not the end, I shall instruct thee in my way. But be true. Would it be hard if I were thy lover, and before thee? But I am thy lover and I am with thee.

25. I shall provide a vessel, when or whence I say not. Seek her not, call her not. Let her declare. Ask nothing. Keep silence. There shall be ordeals.

26. My vessel must be perfect. This is the way of her perfection.

27. The working is of nine moons.

28. The Astarte working, with music and feasting, with wine and all arts of love.

29. Let her be dedicated, consecrated, blood to blood, heart to heart, mind to mind, single in will, none without the circle, all to me.

30. And she shall wander in the witchwood under the Night of Pan, and know the mysteries of the Goat and the Serpent, and of the children that are hidden away.

31. I will provide the place and the material basis, thou the tears and blood.

32. Is it difficult, between matter and spirit? For me it is ecstacy and agony untellable. But I am with thee. I have large strength, have thou likewise.

33. Thou shalt prepare my book for her instruction, also thou shalt teach that she may have captains and adepts in her service. Yea, thou shalt take the black pilgrimage, but it will not be thou that returnest.

34. Let her prepare her work according to my voice in her heart, with thy book as guide, and none other instructing.

35. And let her be in all things wise, and sure, and excellent.

36. But let her think on this: my way is not in the solemn ways, or in the reasoned ways, but in the wild free way of the eagle, and the devious way of the serpent, and the oblique way of the factor unknown and unnumbered.

37. For I am BABALON, and she my daughter, unique, and there shall be no other women like her.

38. In My Name shall she have all power, and all men and excel- lent things, and kings and captains and the secret ones at her command.

39. The first servants are chosen in secret, by my force in her-- a captain, a lawyer, an agitator, a rebel--I shall provide.

40. Call me, my daughter, and I shall come to thee. Thou shalt be full of my force and fire, my passion and power shall surround and inspire thee; my voice in thee shall judge nations.

41. None shall resist thee, whom I lovest. Though they call thee harlot and whore, shameless, false, evil, these words shall be blood in their mouths, and dust thereafter.

42. But my children will know thee and love thee, and this will make them free.

43. All is in thy hands, all power, all hope, all future.

44. One came as a man, and was weak and failed.

45. One came as a woman, and was foolish, and failed.

46. But thou art beyond man and woman, my star is in thee,

and thou shalt avail.

47. Even now thy hour strikes upon the clock of my FATHER. For He prepared a banquet and a Bridal Bed. I was that Bride, appointed from the beginning, as it was written T.O.P.A.N.

48. Now is the hour of birth at hand. Now shall my adept be crucified in the Basilisk abode. 49. Thy tears, thy sweat, thy blood, thy semen, thy love, thy faith shall provide. Ah, I shall drain thee like the cup that is of me, BABALON.

50. Stand thou fast, and I shall pass the first veil to speak with thee, through the stars shake.

51. Stand thou fast, and I shall pass the second veil, while God and Jesus be smitten with the sword of HORUS.

52. Stand thou fast, and I shall pass the third veil, and the shapes of hell shall be turned again to loveliness.

53. For thy sake shall I stride through the flames of Hell, though my tongue be bitten through.

54. Let me behold thee naked and lusting after me, calling upon my name.

55. Let me receive all thy manhood within my Cup, climax upon climax, joy upon joy.

56. Yea, we shall conquer death and Hell together.

57. And the earth is mine.

58. Thou shalt (make the?) Black Pilgrimage.

59. Yea it is even I BABALON and I SHALL BE FREE. Thou fool, be thou also free of sentimentality. Am I thy village queen and thou a sophomore, that thou shouldst have thy nose in my buttocks?

60. It is I, BABALON, ye fools, MY TIME is come, and this my book that my adept prepares is the book of BABALON.

61. Yea, my adept, the Black Pilgrimage. Thou shalt be accursed, and this is the nature of the curse. Thou shalt publish

the secret matter of the adepts thou knowest, witholding no word of it, in an appendix to this my Book. So they shall cry fool, liar, sot, traducer, betrayer. Thou art not glad thou meddled with magick?

62. There is no other way, dear fool, it is the eleventh hour.

63. The seal of my Brother is upon the earth, and His Avatar is before you. There is threshing of wheat and a trampling of grapes that shall not cease until the truth be known unto the least of men.

64. But you who do not accept, you who see beyond, reach out your hands my children and reap the world in the hour of your harvest.

65. Gather together in the covens as of old, whose number is eleven, that is also my number. Gather together in public, in song and dance and festival. Gather together in secret, be naked and shameless and rejoice in my name.

66. Work your spells by the mode of my book, practising secretly, inducing the supreme spell.

67. The work of the image, and the potion and the charm, the work of the spider and the snake, and the little ones that go in the dark, this is your work.

68. Who loves not hates, who hates fears, let him taste fear.

69. This is the way of it, star, star. Burning bright, moon, witch moon.

70. You the secret, the outcast, the accursed and despised, even you that gathered privily of old in my rites under the moon.

71. You the free, the wild, the untamed, that walk now alone and forlorn.

72. Behold, my Brother cracks the world like a nut for your eating.

73. Yea, my Father has made a house for you, and my Mother has prepared a Bridal Bed. My Brother has confounded your enemies.

74. I am the Bride appointed. Come ye to the nuptials--come ye now!

75. My joy is the joy of eternity, and my laughter is the drunken laughter of a harlot in the house of ecstasy.

76. All you loves are sacred, pledge them all to me.

77. Set my star upon your banners and go forward in joy and victory. None shall deny you, and none shall stand before you, because of the Sword of my Brother. Invoke me, call upon me, call me in your convocations and rituals, call upon me in your loves and battles in my name BABALON, wherein is all power given!

And now, please turn over...

The Book of Lilith

~

If you, the reader, have got this far, here's a challenge…

Verses 5-8 of the *Book of Babalon* are missing and presumed lost. Now forget the 73 other statements within this contentious tome. If YOU were channelling Lilith, what four Verses/Utterances would you create for your own, teeny-tiny *Book of Lilith*, in order to change the world for the better?

1.

2.

3.

4.

Answers on a postcard please, or to: alrick13@outlook.com

Printed in Great Britain
by Amazon

36394131R00106